CAMERON JUDD

SHOOTOUT IN DODGE CITY

Book One in the
Carrigan Brothers Series

POCKET **STAR** BOOKS

New York London Toronto Sydney Singapore

An *Original* Publication of POCKET BOOKS

 A Pocket Star Book published by
POCKET BOOKS, a division of Simon & Schuster, Inc.
1230 Avenue of the Americas, New York, NY 10020

ISBN: 0-7434-5708-0

First Pocket Books printing May 2003

10 9 8 7 6 5 4 3 2 1

POCKET STAR BOOKS and colophon are registered trademarks of Simon & Schuster, Inc.

For information regarding special discounts for bulk purchases, please contact Simon & Schuster Special Sales at 1-800-456-6798 or business@simonandschuster.com

Front cover illustration by Bruce Emmett

Printed in the U.S.A.

A ROBBERY IN PROGRESS . . .

Joseph would have enjoyed a good night's rest, but instead he was roaming the streets of Dodge City, looking for his missing brother.

He was near the freight station when he heard something that caught his attention. He could hear the whispers of several male voices, and it didn't take long to ascertain what they were about to do.

"You there!" one of the men said, lifting the shotgun. "You, freeze like a statue."

Joseph didn't freeze but swung around and lifted the pistol. "Town marshal," he lied. "You're under arrest."

The man swore; the shotgun went up a few more inches to his shoulder. . . .

Joseph fired first. The bullet caught the man squarely in the chest and he went down. The sawed-off shotgun went off as he fell, firing into the sky and sounding like a booming cannon in the enclosed alleyway.

Inside the freight office, there was a frenzy of activity and a burst of noise as the burglars reacted to the gunshots. Joseph fired through the big side window and heard the pained grunt of the man who took the bullet, and the dropped—feed-sack thud of his body hitting the floor.

There had been six riders. If this was indeed that same group, there were now only four of them left.

To Katy

1

Abilene, Kansas

A pair of gaudy red shutters hung on spring hinges served in place of the customary bat-wing half doors in the entrance of the Trail's End Saloon. From the boardwalk, Joseph Carrigan peered across the shutter tops into the crowded room beyond. What passed for music blew out against his face like a foul wind: An untuned piano with tacks on its hammers was assaulting a dance tune while a drunken Mexican man with a battered and equally untuned guitar struggled to keep pace.

Joseph shook his head. Terrible, how the unsophisticates of the human race abused the divine gift of music. It was first cousin to blasphemy. But Liam would be drawn to such a place as this, so Joseph pushed through the swinging doors into the musical slaughterhouse. With any luck his brother would be there, and still sober enough to make it back to the hotel on his own.

The saloon reeked of cigar smoke, decomposing spittle in spittoons too long uncleaned, unwashed human bodies, and for some reason onions. Joseph looked around. No Liam.

He eyed the staircase leading up to the floor above. A drunk cowboy was heading up with a rumpled woman in a faded ruffled dress. He hoped Liam wasn't up there, where a man could pick up pestilences not even dreamed of when Adam's curse brought sickness and suffering to the world.

A man weighing at least three hundred pounds perched behind the bar on a stool that strained to hold together under his weight. He looked dull and bored as he wiped out glasses with the corner of his dirty canvas apron.

Joseph approached with a slight smile and a touch of his hat brim. "Good evening, sir. Might I ask a bit of help?"

"I ain't serving. Just wiping glasses."

"I'm not looking for a drink. Just information. I've got a brother, you see, named Liam, and I've lost track of him. He's somewhere in town, and I wondered if maybe you'd seen him in here."

"What kind of name is Liam?"

"Just a name."

"Sounds Irish."

"Yes."

"I don't like Irish."

"I've run across plenty of others who feel the same way."

"Are you Irish?"

"I was raised in Nashville, Tennessee." True, but evasive. Joseph had been raised in Nashville, but Ireland was the land of his birth.

"What's your brother look like?"

"Tall fellow, strong but lean. Dark hair, thick and slightly curly. Eyes blue. Firm chin. Clean-shaven at the moment. Fond of whiskey but only gets drunk when he's worried or angry or sad. He's probably drunk right now. He can have a temper when he's drunk, and gets loud."

"Don't know him. Or maybe I know a hundred men who could be him."

"He wears a gold chain around his neck with a little cross on it. Usually it's hidden beneath his shirt, but sometimes it falls out into view."

Heavy brows lowered disapprovingly. "A man who wears a necklace?"

"It was our mother's, God rest her. He wears it to remind himself of her."

"I ain't seen no man with no necklace."

"There's a gunpowder burn on the left side of his neck. It's been there since he was a boy, ingrained right in the flesh like it was ink. Shaped something like the state of Maine."

The man's blank stare made Joseph wonder if he had even heard of the state of Maine. "Ain't seen him," he said.

"Maybe he's upstairs."

"Ain't nobody like that gone up the stairs tonight."

"Thank you for your time." Joseph touched his hat again and headed for the door.

"Hey," the fat man said.

"Yes?"

"Go look at Flossie's. He might be there."

"Flossie's?"

"One street over. Building with a green door."

"Thank you, sir."

Flossie's was easy to find. The sign above the door billed it as a dance hall, but the females inside struck Joseph as the kind who were probably paid for more than dancing. Two of them approached him with smiles and batting eyes as soon as he'd cleared the door.

"Good evening, sir! Would you like to dance with me?"

"Ma'am, it would be an honor, but my corns are aching this afternoon and I'll have to forgo that pleasure. I'm here in hope of finding my brother."

"If he's as handsome as you, I can tell you he's not here," the second woman said, running her hand lovingly along the lapel of his coat. "Nothing so fine as yourself has come in today."

"He's not nearly so handsome as me," Joseph said. "He is taller, though, and lean. . . ." He gave the same description he'd given the fat barman, including the powder mark on his neck.

"Oh . . . him," the woman said. "Yeah, I seen him."

"Where is he?"

"I don't know. He left after he got stabbed. And he danced a dance with me he hasn't paid for yet. You going to pay it for him?"

"Stabbed?"

"Yeah. Gertie stabbed him."

"Stabbed?"

"That's what I said. You got two bits on you to pay for that dance he owes me for?"

"Why did this Gertie stab my brother?"

"She was drunk."

"So she just stabs folks when she's drunk?"

"She didn't mean to do it. She was trying to stab Mary. Your brother stepped in the way to protect her. Quite a gentleman, but he still owes me for the dance."

"How bad hurt is he?"

"I don't know. He went home with Annie. She was going to patch him up."

"Who's Mary? And who's Annie?"

"Mary is one of our dancing girls. She come in with the gout and said she couldn't dance, so Gertie decided to stab her with her hairpin."

"This Gertie sounds like quite a creature. Now, who's Annie?"

"She's another dancing girl. She was dancing with your brother when Gertie started chasing Mary. He jumped in the way and got stabbed."

"Where does Annie live?"

"Upstairs from the feed store, with her husband. One street over, down a block to the south. But you better hurry."

"Why?"

"I seen Annie's husband heading that direction a few minutes ago. He don't like it when Annie has a man in her house."

"But he's only there for her to patch him up, you said."

"It won't matter to him. He'll never take the time to find out what is really going on."

Joseph touched his hat brim and headed for the door. "One street over, a block to the south, above the feed store. Right?"

"That's right. You can't miss seeing it. You going to pay for that dance?"

Joseph did pay, though even such a minuscule amount wasn't easy to part with just now. "Thank you," he said.

He conducted his search on the run and in fact missed seeing the feed store. No such establishment anywhere. Joseph began to panic. What if Liam got himself killed by some jealous husband, all for no good reason? And how could a jealous husband let his wife work in a dance hall, anyway?

Anger rose with the worry. What was Liam doing, spending money on dance hall girls when their situation was so tight? How much might he have drained today from their meager resources? If he'd played the wastrel, as he had sometimes in the past, Joseph would have his hide!

Why was it that Liam always made the most imprudent choices in any given situation? He'd been like that since he was little, and Joseph was tired of it. This time he'd not let it pass.

Maybe the feed store was farther down the street. He ran on, dodging around a woman who stepped out of a dress shop at just the wrong moment. He missed her but trod on her toes. He spun around to apologize, backing away from her as he did so, and collided blindly with a man coming out of a tobacco shop beside the dress store. The man went down and Joseph barely avoided doing so himself.

"What the devil, young man!" Joseph's victim declared. "Watch where you're going!"

Joseph rushed to help the man up. "I'm sorry, sir. My fault . . . I do apologize."

The frowning man pulled free of Joseph's grasp and dusted himself off. "Good thing for you you didn't crush my new cigars."

"I'm mighty sorry."

"Why are you going in such a reckless way down a public thoroughfare?"

"I'm trying to find my brother. I've heard he's hurt and was told he is being cared for somewhere on this street, in rooms above some feed store."

"The feed store? Oh, yes. Down yonder."

"Where?"

The man pointed. "That place."

"I don't see it."

"There! Right there! Don't you see?"

Just then a second-story window three buildings down, on the far side of the street, exploded outward under the force of the human form that burst through it and tumbled to the street in a jumble of flailing arms and legs, broken glass, splintered wood, and billowing dust.

"I'll be confounded!" the man with the cigars said. "Who the devil —"

"Not the devil," Joseph said, "but close enough. It's my brother."

He loped across the street toward Liam's crumpled, glass-covered form.

2

Liam pushed himself up slowly, grimacing, then rolled over and sat amid the shattered glass, rubbing the back of his neck. Attracted by his rather dramatic plunge to the street, people stared from the boardwalk and assorted doors and windows.

Liam looked up as Joseph reached him. "Hello, Joseph."

"Liam, are you hurt?"

"I don't know. I don't think so. I can still wiggle my toes."

"You'll be hurt when I get through with you. Are you drunk?"

Liam mumbled something noncommittal in his low, somewhat gravelly voice. Joseph sniffed the air; he could detect the scent of whiskey wafting up from his brother's person.

"You sorry, worthless, wasteful, drunken son of a—"

"Careful, brother," Liam interrupted. "That's our sainted mother you're about to insult."

A man appeared in the ruined and vacant window from which Liam had plunged. "That'll learn you!" he bellowed. "You come around here again, you'll get worse!"

Liam looked up. "You come down here, you bastard, and I'll give you worse right now!"

Joseph could have swallowed his tongue. "Liam, just how big a fool are you? You're in no shape to fight!"

The man was no longer in the window. They could hear his heavy footfalls from inside the thin-walled building as he lumbered down the stairs. Liam tried to get up, winced, and slumped down again. "You're right. I guess you'll have to fight him for me."

"Oh, sweet mother of—"

Liam looked up sharply, bleary eyes widening. "Watch out, Joseph—blasphemy! You don't do that, remember?"

Joseph, overcome with frustration, did something that surprised him as much as it did Liam: He drew back his foot and gave Liam a fairly sound kick that hit him first in the arm, then grazed off to the side and caught him above the kidney. Liam grunted loudly. He'd been propping himself with the arm and it gave way, so that he collapsed back onto the street.

All of this happened just as the big man from upstairs reached the door and came out with murder in his eye. He glared at Liam and advanced toward him.

Joseph stepped into his path. "Hold up, sir. Let's talk about this."

"Who the hell are you?"

"Joseph Carrigan. I'm the brother of this wretch you just threw out the window."

"Step aside."

"As much as I'd enjoy seeing him get what he's due, I can't do that. He's my brother."

"He messed with my wife. I'll kill any man who does that!"

"I didn't mess with her," Liam said. "She gave me some bread and jam, that's all."

Both men ignored him. "I understand how you feel," Joseph said to the angry man. "But this is one man you won't kill. Not without going through me first."

The big fellow roared, cursed, and cocked a fist that to Joseph appeared to be the size of a millstone. Joseph reacted swiftly. His right arm blurred in motion as his own fist drove up and in once, twice, three times, hitting the man twice in the chin and once on the forehead. He staggered back, arms windmilling, collapsed onto his rump, then tilted to the right and sank onto the ground.

"Good work, Joseph," Liam said. "Except I think you've killed him."

Joseph feared the same. He'd hit the man harder

than he'd planned, and now he didn't appear to be moving or breathing. Then, thankfully, he gave a great heave and gasped loudly. He still lay there mostly senseless, but he was alive.

Joseph shook his numbed fist and rubbed his knuckles on his pants. Somebody among the observers hollered out praise for his pugilistic skill, but Joseph sensed that most would have liked to have seen the fellow get to Liam and work him over. Joseph himself was not entirely hostile to their sentiment.

"Come on, you troublesome worm," Joseph said to Liam without the slightest trace of warmth. "Let's get out of here before he comes around."

"Thank you for what you did."

"Shut up and get on your feet."

"Give me a hand."

Joseph swore beneath his breath, reached down, took Liam's hand, and pulled upward. Liam came up clumsily, groaning, and steadied himself. His shirt was bloodied, as were his lip and his hands.

From the crowd of onlookers a woman's voice wailed and sobbed, accusing Joseph of killing the man he'd hit.

"He's not dead, ma'am," Joseph replied. To Liam he whispered out of the side of his mouth: "Come on. Let's get away from here before some wandering town deputy comes around the corner and starts asking questions."

They headed off together, moving as fast as Liam's battered condition would allow. Behind them the crowd gathered around the fallen man, who was beginning to sit up. The man's wife appeared in the doorway of the building, actually looking disappointed to see that her husband was still among the living.

"You are truly an infuriating man, Liam," Joseph said. "You'll get us both killed someday. 'Jam and bread.' I never heard it called that before."

"I'm serious, Joseph. That's all I was doing: sitting at her table, eating jam and bread while she made over me for having gotten stabbed."

"With a hairpin? Not exactly a real stabbing."

"Hey, you don't know how bad it hurt. I thought I'd come out of my own skin."

"I'm just grateful you still had your pants on when you came out that window."

"Joseph, listen to me: bread and jam. That's all. Real bread, real jam. Everybody was clothed."

"And if the husband hadn't come back?"

Liam shrugged and said nothing.

"Just what I thought."

"I guess Mother looks down from above in great pride at her fine, moral-minded, straight-and-narrow–walking Joseph."

"Let's just hope she doesn't see her other son."

"Hell with you."

"Just shut up."

"You act like an old woman. What makes you like you are?"

"Shut up about that. Tell me how much money you spent."

"No. You tell me why you're so high-and-mighty moral about women and such. You weren't like that when we were younger. Then you come back from the war all holy as a priest. What happened to make you like that?"

"Tell me how much you spent, because we don't have money to waste. We hardly have enough to survive."

"You tell me why you act like you do and then we'll talk about how much I spent. Tell me what happened to change you!"

"We're not talking about me. I'm not the problem here: You're the problem—you and your complete lack of any sense or restraint."

"Come on, Joseph. Tell me!"

"Nothing to tell. How much did you spend?"

"Tell me!"

Joseph leaned into Liam's face and all but shouted: "All right, I'll tell you, damn it! I'll tell you what it's like to stand in the rain looking down at . . ."

Liam stared into his brother's face, waiting. But Joseph said no more, only stared back.

Liam shook his head. "You did it again. Almost said

something, then held it back. What is it you won't tell me?"

Joseph's face reddened; a vein in his temple bulged visibly. He glared at Liam, then with effort swallowed hard and got control of his temper. Joseph didn't get mad often. Whenever he did, it was usually because of Liam.

"There's no more to say, Liam, except that your inability to keep your hands off women almost got you killed. That was quite a fall you took."

"Why, I fell ten feet farther than that three times in one summer when we were boys. Remember that? That big maple I was bound and determined to climb to the top of, no matter what?"

"I remember."

"I never did make it to the top of that tree. It still bothers me after all these years. Maybe someday I'll go back and try it again, if the tree's still there."

"Right now you can't afford to go back, Liam. We've got very little between us and destitution. Yet, you went off drinking and dancing. That's what galls me: the foolishness of it."

"Joseph, sometimes a man has to spit in the face of fate. Sometimes he has to shake himself loose and enjoy himself just so he can bear his burdens a little better. Sometimes doing something foolish is the most sensible thing a man can do."

Joseph shook his head. "I never heard such non-sense."

"Tell me this: Was it me or you who insisted on renting a hotel room, even though we can't justify the cost?"

"It was me."

"Tell me *that* wasn't foolish!"

"It wasn't: It was shelter. Shelter is a necessity. Drinking and dancing and 'toast-and-jamming' with another man's wife is foolish."

"We can't afford the hotel room."

"I know. Which is why we'll not be spending another night there after this one."

Liam paused, twisted from side to side, and made the face of a man with a sore back. "I think I might have stove myself up in that fall."

"You're lucky you didn't hit on your head and die."

"The Lord looks after fools like me."

"Which explains how you survived the war."

"No. I survived the war because folks like you were on the other side."

Joseph smiled feebly but said nothing. He knew what Liam was doing: He was trying to steer them away from their argument, which was of course to his advantage in that he held the weaker side of the dispute. It was difficult indeed to justify drinking and dancing and womanizing when they were a hair's breadth from bankruptcy. And it was still only afternoon! Had he not been thrown from a window, Liam probably would have kept going well into the night.

Joseph decided to let the argument end. It was pointless to argue with Liam, anyway. Besides, he had a point about the hotel room. They really shouldn't have rented it. Maybe the hotel was Joseph's way of giving one final shake of the fist at bad fortune.

"Joseph, what will we do about supper?"

"I don't know. What had you planned to have for supper before you got tossed out a window?"

"Whiskey."

"Well, I guess you'll just have to get by on the bread and jam you already ate."

Liam grunted and looked sourly away.

They walked the rest of the way to the hotel without further words.

Liam slept and Joseph sat slumped in a chair in the corner of the second-floor hotel room, staring at him and at the moment actually envying him. Liam was sleeping, oblivious to the world. No worries, no pains, no fears about what would happen to them next.

For the moment Joseph was left to carry their mutual burdens alone.

It was not supposed to have happened as it did. In their grand scheme, at this point they were to have been celebrating the success of their cattle drive, flush with money, wearing fine suits and making great plans for their next, even bigger venture. The gamble was to have paid off big. Liam and Joseph Carrigan, according to the plan, were to have been strutting right now.

Unexpectedly, Liam rolled over and looked at his brother. "Sorry I did what I did."

Joseph shrugged.

"Just trying to forget about how bad it all fell apart, that's all I was doing. I figured, what was one afternoon of cutting loose going to hurt? Otherwise, there's nothing to do but sit around and fret."

"I know."

"We've lost it all this time, brother."

"No we haven't. Just go on to sleep."

"We *have* lost it. Right now we've got less than when we started the cattle drive."

"I know, but at least we've got something. And there's always a way to rebuild."

Liam grinned, but it was a sad and weary grin. "How could so many things go wrong on one cattle drive? It just ain't possible, Joseph."

"I wouldn't have thought so."

"What will we do?"

"I don't know. Yet."

"You're a good man, Joseph. A decent, Christian fellow. Hell, you even go to Mass. The Lord will listen to you. Say some prayers about us, would you? Ask him to send us some better luck."

"I've already prayed that prayer."

"Good." Liam rolled over again. In a few moments he was snoring.

Joseph watched him a minute or two, then stood, put on his hat, and went out for a long walk in the waning light of an ending day.

What would they do, indeed?

Joseph could not answer Liam's question, and it gnawed at him. He had always prided himself on his ability to come up with a plan. Since boyhood he'd been the one who could make things work out. The pathfinder. The escape artist.

"The clever one," his father used to describe him when comparing him to his brother. "The deft one . . . the mouse who always gets out of the trap. Liam, now . . . Liam's the big, clumsy rat who stumbles into the trap to begin with and tries to fight his way out of it. To be sure, it's good he's got Joseph to look out for him."

Joseph was glad his father couldn't see them now. He'd not be so quick to praise Joseph's cleverness this time. It was Joseph's scheming and planning that had gotten them into this situation. And it was proving hard to find a way out of the trap.

They had invested all they had in the cattle drive. They'd hired several carefully chosen men to herd the cattle and a cook to feed them all. Joseph had taken every precaution. He'd even bought some basic physician's supplies and taken along a medical book so he could deal with any injuries that came up.

They'd been ready for anything and everything. And anything and everything was just what they had received.

Storms, stampedes, injuries, even a death when one of their cowboys got drunk on whiskey he'd sneaked along in his saddlebag—strictly against the rules—and rode over the edge of a bluff. There had been sickness among the cattle, then among the men. Rustlers struck, successfully. One of their hired hands stole from his peers and sneaked away, and two others went after him, abandoning the drive and leaving them badly shorthanded. Another, a true coward named Mack Stanley, took a dislike to Liam and tried to ambush him. He failed, and Liam beat him nearly senseless, then sent him packing. Mack Stanley vowed revenge but showed few signs he would ever find the courage to actually seek it. Liam told him he'd meet him anytime, anyplace, and on any terms he wished.

Then, to cap off the run of boundless disasters, the cook managed somehow to serve up bad stew that left the entire crew too ill to continue, losing precious days. Then another stampede—perhaps caused by Mack Stanley, though they had no solid proof—and the loss of more cattle. Even the cattle they saved shed precious pounds from the exertion of the stampede, declining in marketability with every pound they dropped.

The drive had been intended to make the Carrigan brothers a hefty profit. Instead, they'd barely been able to pay off their hands. They ended up with less money than they'd started out with.

They'd failed before, more than once, but this time they'd failed magnificently. Joseph did not feel clever anymore. He wondered if Liam would come to despise him again, as he had a couple of times before in their somewhat turbulent lives. Because the cattle drive had been Joseph's idea.

Joseph found a café and ordered himself a cup of coffee. He wasn't a drinker, found alcohol loathsome, but he did love his coffee. Surely even an impoverished loser had the right to enjoy a hot cup of Arbuckles' while he stood on the deck and watched the vessel of his life sink deeper into the dark waters, moment by moment.

What will we do?

Liam's question haunted him. Joseph stared at the sunset out the checkerboard-paned café window, unsure whether this time he'd be able to find an answer.

He tossed coins onto the table and left to roam the streets again.

His deft mind wasn't functioning very well today. Maybe Liam had the right idea. Embrace your misfortune. Dull its pain with whiskey . . . while you can still afford whiskey. Distract yourself with dance hall women. Escape the world and its problems in a drunken stupor.

No, Joseph thought. *Not me. There's always something that can be done. Even in the darkest forest there's always a path that leads out. If you can find it.*

Joseph kept walking, his mind working frantically, searching for the outbound path but finding nothing.

3

The man was painting a wall by lantern light. He was short, slightly round, and perched very precariously on a ladder that had seen better days. Joseph glanced at him as he wandered past, preoccupied, and gave him little heed. Moments later, however, the sound of a tremendous crash made Joseph turn just in time to see the ladder fall to the ground like felled timber, sending the man tumbling, arms and legs going everywhere and brown paint cascading all around.

Joseph went over to help the fellow up, stepping over a puddle of paint. "Are you hurt, sir?"

The man got upright with the aid of Joseph's extended hand and checked himself over. "I seem to be no worse for the misadventure," he said. "My ladder's done for, though. Broke like a toothpick, and me on it!"

"You've lost a couple of gallons of paint, it appears."

"Yes, indeed. Ah, well. I was tired of painting, and

it's nearly too dark to see what I was doing, anyway. That lantern is no better than my ladder was."

Joseph looked the fellow over. The man had a plain, appealing face and cheerful demeanor. He was dressed in rough, ragged clothing. Joseph wasn't sure, but he thought he detected hints of an Irish brogue in his speech.

"I'm astonished, sir," Joseph said. "Paint is everywhere, but not a drop on you. By all rights you should have been coated with the stuff."

The man looked down at his slightly plump self. "Well! You're right! It appears I've been divinely protected, eh? Goes with the profession, perhaps." He chuckled, then noted Joseph's lack of comprehension. "Oh, but you don't know what I mean, with me dressed in these clothes. These are my painting clothes, sir. Castoffs left behind by a man down on his luck, who I was able to clothe a bit better from the church community collection box. Normally I'd be in my collar and suit, looking much more like a priest than I do now. I am Father James Rath." He winked. " 'The Rath of God,' I like to call myself. Quite pleased to meet you." He thrust out his hand.

Joseph shook it. "Joseph Carrigan. Pleased to meet you, Father." He glanced at the building Rath had been painting. It was a small church. Joseph had been so preoccupied with his own thoughts that he hadn't even noticed that as he passed it.

"Carrigan, eh? Good Irish name."

"Indeed. Though I find at times a good Irish name can be an impediment to progress in this nation."

"Oh, don't I know what you mean! We Irish, we have to scrap and fight our way through, no doubt about it! But He likes the Irish, I think," Rath said, pointing toward the sky. "How else can you explain me escaping every splash of paint, eh?" Rath laughed heartily, and Joseph instantly liked the man. He reminded him of a friendly shopkeeper he'd known back when he was growing up in Nashville.

But suddenly the priest grew a bit more serious. He lifted a finger and gently shook it at Joseph. "What you say about the Irish in this nation is true, but no whining about it, eh? That does no good at all. And many have it far worse than we Irish."

"Of course."

"Be proud of your heritage, I always say. God gave it to you, after all."

"Yes. And some He also gives noses that are too big or ears that look like wings. We're all left to get on as best we can with what we're given, and what we're not. As for my heritage, I'm not ashamed of it. But I don't wear it like a fancy coat, for it just hampers a man's chances. Thank God, I didn't pick up my father's brogue."

"Your father is a born Irishman?"

"He was. In fact, so am I, and my brother too."

"Why no brogue, then?"

"We were brought to this nation as very small children after my mother died. Liam and I were raised in Nashville. Father wouldn't let us pick up his ways of speech. It would keep us from succeeding in America, he believed. I remember seeing him whip Liam one time for beginning to speak like an Irishman. Father was deadly serious about Americanizing us. He wanted to change our surname at one point, and Liam's Christian name as well, but we raised such a fuss that he relented."

Father Rath shook his head sadly. "I understand your father's thinking, but it is a wretched thing to feel such a way about your native land."

"Oh, he loved his native land: He pined for it all his days. But his native land didn't love him."

"How so?"

"He came to this country because he had to. Trouble back home . . . a fiery temper, a bit too much to drink one night. My father was a big, strong man, and when he struck with that fist of his, he struck like a hammer."

The priest lifted one brow, just barely. "Hard enough, perhaps, to kill a man?"

"Yes. Hard enough to kill a man dead as a stone right on the tavern floor. A man who was the son of the richest and most unforgiving man within a hundred miles."

"Ah! Enough to put anyone to flight."

"A man does what he must, and my father did. He had a brother, Patrick, older than him by two years. Patrick had a wanderlust and had gone on to America some years earlier and settled in Nashville—doing precisely what, the family really wasn't certain. In any case, when Father found his troubles in Ireland, he decided the prudent thing to do was come to America himself, find Patrick, and try to stay out of pub fights from then on."

Rath nodded. "This is an intriguing conversation, Mr. Carrigan. And all the better if we had a bite of cake to go with it. And coffee as well."

"I just had coffee, but more wouldn't be unwelcome. And I've yet to turn down the offer of cake."

"My house is right there, the little clapboard one. Come join me for a bite and tell me more of yourself and your family."

Joseph found it all somewhat unreal at first, sitting in the parlor of the humble home of a priest, eating cake like some society woman at tea and talking about his family background. It felt a bit like confession, without the personal embarrassment.

But that wasn't fully accurate. The longer Joseph talked, the more evident it became that his family history had more than its share of failure in it. Theirs was a saga of that great success always just ahead but never quite present, of fortunes nearly won but, in the end, not won.

His father hadn't even succeeded in finding his own brother, the very man he'd traveled to America to join.

"How hard did he search?" Rath asked.

"In the beginning, when it was a matter of shoe leather and asking questions, he searched very hard. But all he was able to find out was that Patrick Carrigan had left Nashville and gone west—nobody knew quite where—to seek better fortunes. He'd left in a hurry and had said little. . . . There was talk that a woman and an angry husband might have been involved, giving him some motivation not to say much."

"Ah. I see."

"It was something like my father's own situation, I suppose: fleeing one place to leave behind trouble and—you hope—find something better."

"Did your father consider following Patrick west?"

"There was no track to follow. Patrick had vanished like smoke. Eventually, Father gave up trying to find him and believed he might be dead. He forgot about him. Worked in the meatpacking business until he'd worked himself into his own grave, but he raised Liam and me. That was his story. Nothing to show at the end of his days except two sons, neither of whom has managed to do the family name very proud."

Rath took a sip of coffee. "Perhaps you've done

better than you believe. You've managed to stay together and work as a family team. That alone is of value, is it not?"

"It is. But we've had our divisions in the past. Liam and I were torn apart for a few years by two situations: a woman, and the late war."

"Opposite sides, perhaps?"

"Yes, as regards the war. I favored the Union and headed into the loyalist regions in east Tennessee to do my part. Liam followed the majority in Nashville in favoring the Confederacy. As I look back at it, I can see that us splitting apart that way wasn't caused as much by honest convictions as the fact we already hated each other because of Rachel White."

"The woman."

"Yes. We both wanted her, very much. Vied for her, competed, came to blows a time or two. In the end it wound up she was simply having some fun watching us make fools of ourselves. She married a butcher and moved to Atlanta. By then Liam and I were so hateful toward each other that the war provided a handy reason to go separate ways."

"How did you come back together?"

"The hand of God, I've come to believe."

"Ah! Just my cup of tea. Aren't I the perfect audience to hear such a thing! Pray continue."

"It was all very unlikely, on the surface. . . . That's what I mean by the hand of God being involved. Liam and I actually met on the battlefield: Stones River. Both of us were separated from our units, isolated . . . we met in a grove of trees by a little creek, the battle raging all around, and almost shot each other before we each realized who the other was. We laid down our rifles and stared at each other for a minute or so, then I burst out laughing and Liam broke down crying. Then he laughed and I cried. Then we both laughed. We sat down together and talked, believe it or not—just talked to one another and ignored all the fighting. Amazing we weren't both killed."

"The hand of God again, I'd say," Rath said around a bite of cake.

"I would agree. Liam probably would not. He's not a faith-filled man. It's been fifteen years or so since he's so much as spoken to a priest, much less made confession, gone to Mass, and the like."

"Skeptical? Intellectual barriers?"

Joseph chuckled. "No. Not Liam. An unwillingness to give up his occasional sinful pleasures. That's what it is in his case."

"In most cases, I would say. Stubborn self-will. That's what keeps most from faith. But that's for a sermon later on, not this conversation. Tell me what happened after you reunited."

"We talked in that grove of trees and realized that the things that had driven us apart didn't matter anymore. Our father had died while we were both away at war, in theory trying to kill each other, and I think that sobered us both. Neither of us had any other family in this country except each other. We realized we needed to stick together, like Father had raised us to do. He died a sad man because his sons were divided against each other."

"Did you ever hear from the woman again?"

"No, and good riddance. We laughed at the fools we'd let her make of us. We talked of how neither of us cared anymore about the war—didn't really even care who won or lost, as long as it ended. We shook hands, vowed to find one another after the war, and made arrangements to meet back in Nashville in the same neighborhood in which we'd grown up. Then we went back into the battle and spent the rest of the war doing our best to stay alive. When it was over, I headed back to Nashville and found Liam already there. We've not been separated since."

"What brought you west?"

"Failure. Liam and I have been shopkeepers, stock-yard operators, housepainters, barn builders . . . Nothing has succeeded. We eventually did what every failure in America does: headed west to see if we could find better fortunes on the far side of the Mississippi."

"And have you?"

"Father, we just completed the most devastatingly unsuccessful cattle drive in the history of this nation.

We are very nearly wiped out, have no means to rebuild, and Liam seems ready to drink himself to death and be done with it. I don't know what will come next for us."

Father Rath took that in with a thoughtful frown. He set down his cup and steepled his fingers before his face, thinking deeply.

"You have no living kin in this nation who can help you?" he asked at length.

"No. Not unless my uncle Patrick is still out there somewhere."

"Might he be?"

"Well . . ." Joseph paused, then reached into an inside vest pocket and pulled out a small leather wallet. From it he produced a very yellowed piece of newspaper, folded and ragged around the edges. He handed it to the priest, who took up reading glasses from a nearby desk, settled them on his nose, and read.

He looked up, slipping the glasses off. "Interesting! Where did you get this clipping?"

"I found it inside an old trunk that someone had left along the trail back in Texas. Some family moving from one place to another, I guess. The trunk was empty but it had been lined with newspaper. When I looked inside, my uncle's name all but jumped off the page at me. I tore out that part of the newspaper lining and kept it."

"Do you and Liam think this Patrick Carrigan is your uncle?"

"Liam doesn't even know about that clipping. I never showed it to him—thought he'd scoff at it, for some reason. And I honestly don't know if it is the same man. There's nothing given about his age, his looks, his family. Just the name . . . and the fact he almost beat a man to death in a saloon. And that, I admit, does sound like my family."

"How old would your uncle be now?"

"In his fifties—a young fellow by my family's standards. The Carrigans are all strapping, healthy men. My grandfather was in good health all the way into his nineties, then died one night in his sleep. That's the way it usually goes in my family: good health, long life, and a quick, easy death."

"One could have it much worse than that, eh?"

"Oh, yes. I've always thought it was God's recompense. He gives my people long life and an easy death in compensation for lack of funds."

The priest chuckled. "One never knows why such things happen. Perhaps you're right." He studied the newspaper clipping once more, flipped it over, and scanned the back of it. "Interesting. If I were in your shoes, I believe I'd be inclined to investigate that."

"How? I don't even know what newspaper this came from. I don't know how old the story is, or if this Pat Carrigan is my uncle at all."

"Oh, I can tell you what newspaper that came from."

"How?"

"From the apothecary advertisement on the back of the clipping. I know the place. And if the man in your story is your uncle, you may be much closer to him than you think."

4

Morning came, spilling through the window sunlight, which was most unwelcome to Liam. He opened his eyes, groaned, and squeezed them closed again. The light still bothered him, so he rolled over, in the process catching a glimpse of Joseph still in the overstuffed chair in which he'd slept away the night.

Joseph was awake now, looking at Liam with a brightness in his eyes that was almost as obnoxious as the light shining through the window.

"Good morning, Liam. I was wondering when you'd wake up."

Liam said nothing. Not even a grunt.

"It's getting a little late. Wake up: We need to talk."

Liam made a low, barely audible grumbling noise somewhere deep in his throat.

Joseph stood up and went to the bedside and looked down at Liam, who responded by pulling the covers over his head.

"Come on, Liam. Hang it all, wake up! I've got news."

"Go tell it to the newspaper. I'll read it later."

"You feeling all right?"

"Go away."

"You did get thrown out of a window, after all."

"Damn it, Joseph!"

"I'll go down to the café, get you a cup of coffee, and bring it up."

Liam didn't want coffee, just sleep. But somewhere in his clouded mind enough reason stirred to make him realize that Joseph fetching coffee meant Joseph out of the room for a few minutes. "Go ahead," he mumbled.

"Black?"

"Ummph."

Taking that as an affirmative, Joseph left the room, closing the door too loudly—on purpose—making Liam cuss softly before quickly falling asleep again. It seemed only moments later when the door reopened and Joseph returned with a tray laden with two china cups and a crockery pot full of steaming coffee. There were also biscuits and butter.

The aromas usually would have wakened Liam's appetite, but he'd drunk so much the day before that food was repulsive. He rolled over again, suffered another assault of sunlight, and with a muttered oath gave up the fight and accepted the brutal inevitability of morning and waking up. He rolled onto his back, eyes closed and mouth open, and flung his arms to the side, palms toward the ceiling.

"I can't believe you're the same man who would roll out of his bedding even before the cook sang out, back during the cattle drive," Joseph said.

"Throw those biscuits out the window. The smell of them makes me sick." Liam's throat was scratchy, his voice a rasp.

"I'm going to eat them. You don't want one, I gather."

"God, no."

Joseph buttered his biscuit, poured coffee, and began to eat slowly and with obvious enjoyment. Liam glared at him sidewise through eyes like slits.

"If I'd bought those biscuits, you'd declare it a foolish waste of money."

"A man has to eat."

"I wish you'd do it somewhere else and let me sleep."

Joseph, enjoying the suffering he was inflicting, shrugged and kept on eating. He slurped the coffee very loudly.

A minute passed and a little more life crept into Liam Carrigan's body. He plumped up his pillow and propped himself up slightly. "I'll have some coffee, I reckon."

Joseph poured him a cupful. Liam took only a small

sip, then sat up, holding the cup on his lap. "Why are you so full of sunshine this morning?"

"Didn't know I was."

"You're grinning while you eat that smelly biscuit. What did you say about news?"

"Remember that prayer you asked me to pray?"

"No."

"Sure you do. Well, it got answered."

Liam said, "Mine didn't. Turtledove McGee wasn't lying beside me when I woke up."

"Forget her. She's married, fat, and has whelped at least three times, last I heard. Liam, I know what we're going to do. I think I know the destiny that has been planned for us."

Liam was fast growing tired of talking. His headache was worsening. "Go on. I'll just listen."

Joseph hopped up from his chair and began pacing back and forth as he spoke, his coffee cup sloshing. The pacing annoyed Liam, but he said nothing.

"You know what people say about ghosts, Liam? How they are people who have died with unfinished business, things they intended to do but didn't? So they fail to die the way a person is supposed to, and end up lingering around, failures in life and failures in death?"

"Unhh."

"We're ghosts, Liam. You and me."

"Then go rattle your chain at somebody else."

"What I mean is, we've got an unfinished task. Our

schemes have failed us because we haven't finished what we were supposed to do—what we came to this country to do. Once that is done, we'll be able to succeed."

Liam finally took another sip from his rapidly cooling cup. "You're babbling."

"No. I'm more clearheaded than I've been in months."

"So what are we supposed to do?"

"Find our uncle Patrick. Fulfill our quest."

Liam slowly turned his head to give his brother the closest thing to a withering stare that he could generate. "You woke me up for this?"

Joseph paced faster beside the bed. "I've been talking to a priest, Liam. I think it was one of those divine appointments. All the things that have happened to us have been designed to lead us here to this place, at this time, so that I would meet Father Rath and receive the guidance we need."

Liam had heard this kind of thing since he was a boy. Joseph had a long history of finding mystical significance, signs, and portents in almost every event, from stomachaches to thunderstorms. Liam recalled a comment their late father had made to him in private: "Every time Joseph hears somebody belch, he thinks the voice of God just spoke to him."

"Joseph the Dreamer," their father had sometimes called his son when he wasn't around.

"Why did you go to a priest?"

"I didn't; I encountered him by chance. We fell to talking, and he's the one who made it all come clear for me."

Liam glared. "Well, let me muddy it up again. Our own father couldn't find Patrick, not even a footprint to follow. He finally decided he was probably dead. Do you know something new that changes that?"

"I . . . I just have the strongest sense that it's what we are supposed to do."

"We don't know where to look. Warm up this coffee, would you?"

"That's not entirely true. There is one thing." He poured Liam's coffee, then produced the newspaper scrap he'd shown Father Rath. "His name is in this newspaper story. At least, it could be him. There can't be all that many Patrick Carrigans roaming the country, I don't think."

With aching eyes, Liam read the clipping silently, turned it over and glanced at the back of it, then read it again. He handed it back to Joseph, who had braced himself for a strong negative reaction. Surprisingly, Liam didn't give one.

"So maybe Patrick is alive after all," he said.

"I have the strongest feeling it's him. And that we have to find him. It's an issue of destiny . . . doing what we were meant to do."

"Where'd you get that piece of newspaper?"

"You remember that old trunk we found lying out by the trail? It was part of the lining."

"It doesn't say when or where it was printed."

"Actually, it does, in a way. Father Rath noted it. There's a business name on the back of the clipping: Dellworth Apothecary. He recognized it. It's in Dodge City and was built within the past three years. So that was probably printed in Dodge sometime within that same period."

Liam frowned, thinking. "We're not that far away from there."

"No. It's an opportunity, Liam. We might actually have a chance to do what our father never could. We've got enough money to get us by for a little while. We've got our horses. We could go to Dodge City, see what we can learn, and if we're lucky we might even find Patrick."

Liam cleared his throat, finally getting rid of most of the raspiness. His headache was terrible and hurt most when he spoke, but with Joseph in a talking mood he might as well just resign himself and bear the pain. "If they haven't hanged him. It says he nearly beat a man to death."

"All the more reason to believe this is the right Patrick Carrigan. All our kin back home were scrappers with hot tempers. Father always said Patrick was just like them, quick to fight."

Liam scooted up a little higher and leaned back

against the headboard. "It can't hurt to go to Dodge. We've got nothing else to do."

Joseph wondered why he was meeting so little resistance, then recalled Dodge's reputation as a western Babylon: Liam's kind of town. Of course he'd not argue against going there. Joseph gave a deliberately understated reply. "It's certainly worth checking into."

"What about money?"

"We'll find work. Getting-by work. I'll dump and wash slop jars if I have to. But it says that Patrick Carrigan is a cattleman. Did you note that? So if we actually find him, there may be work with him for us. The Carrigan family back together again."

Liam mulled it over, but he was thinking as much about Dodge City's saloons as anything. "I'm inclined to say yes. We've got nothing better. Can you pull those curtains closed for me?" He closed his eyes, head throbbing from extended talk. His back hurt, too, wrenched during the fall from the window.

"Close them yourself. This is all fine, Liam. There's destiny at work here! Think about this: Of all the people who could have found that trunk on the trail, it was me. Of all the names that could have been in the newspapers lining the trunk, it was that of Patrick Carrigan. Then I chance to stumble across a priest just because he spills his paint bucket, and he is able to give us our first clue ever about where Patrick might be—or at least where he might have been a year or two ago. Is it

all really coincidence? Or is this something we're supposed to do?"

Liam wondered why Joseph was still trying to persuade him to do something he'd just agreed to do
already. Joseph had that habit—just another thing to
make him more annoying. And Liam could have easily
answered the philosophical question Joseph posed.
Although it was Joseph who fancied himself the
philosopher of the family, Liam had the common sense
to know that it was easy to find signs and portents to
take one in any direction one might want to go. He put
little stock in Joseph's attempts to mystify this situation.

But it wouldn't hurt to do what Joseph had in mind.
Clearly they had to find work somewhere, and it might
as well be Dodge City, a place where a man could enjoy
himself. And they'd be no worse off by pursuing this
newspaper clipping lead, meager as it was. With a possible clue in hand for the first time, they had an obliga-
tion to investigate it at least.

"Why did you wait until now to show me that newspaper scrap?" Liam asked.

"I thought you'd be unimpressed with it—maybe
think me foolish for finding any significance in it.
Besides, we had plenty of troubles at that time that
seemed more worthy of attention."

"It can't hurt to go to Dodge City and ask a few questions."

"Thank you for agreeing to this, Liam. I'd expected you to argue with me."

"I'm too sore and sick to argue," he said. "Danged if my tooth ain't starting to hurt too. I felt it when the coffee hit it. Hell, the last thing I need is a toothache. When do we have to be out of this room?"

"Ten o'clock."

Liam grunted, set his coffee cup on the bed table, and sank down low into the bed again, burying himself in the covers, determined not to rise for another hour. Joseph, excited by merely having a plan for their immediate future, finished his breakfast, put on his hat, and left to have a morning walk.

5

They rode side by side along a dirt road winding toward Dodge, examining the landscape and wondering what they would find ahead. If asked, they would have given two different answers. *The fulfillment of our destiny and the door that will open onto a reunion of the Carrigan clan in America,* Joseph would have replied. *Nothing but some good saloons, loud dance halls, and some mighty pretty women of the sort who don't attend Sunday school,* Liam would have replied.

Ford County, Kansas. A county now six years old and best known for its most famous town, Dodge City. Dodge, as it was generally called for short, had become a legally organized entity a year after the county itself had, although the town had been around longer in a more informal sense, thanks to the buffalo hunters who had first frequented the vicinity. There were fewer than a thousand permanent residents in Dodge, Joseph had been told back in Abilene, but the population of course grew during the cattle season as trail-weary cowboys arrived. Its reputation as a rowdy town was due to the cowboys, for the most part, not the full-time residents.

Secretly, Joseph worried some about the timing of their arrival. They were reaching Dodge at its wildest season. Plenty of temptations for Liam would be at hand, and Joseph did not expect him to put forth the effort to resist them.

Ford County, named for an old Kansas cavalryman, struck both the Carrigan brothers as an appealing place. It was scarce on timber—what there was was mostly box elders and cottonwoods—but there was good building stone to be had in certain parts, and the land was generally level and easily traversed. That pleased cattlemen. The Arkansas River watered the county and accounted for the fact that about twenty percent of Ford County was bottomland, and that pleased agrarians.

The day was clear, the weather pleasantly cool. Joseph was in a good mood, invigorated by the nip in the air and the fact they would come in sight of Dodge by sunset. He talked a lot, as he was prone to do at such times. Liam just listened and noted he was thirsty—the kind of thirst water would not suffice to quench. He was worried too. The tooth that had started to hurt back in Abilene was worse now. It probably merited a pulling, but that raised the terrifying prospect of a dental visit. He kept as a protected secret the fact that dentists gave him cold shudders. He'd survived war, poverty, various illnesses, but the thought of going to a dentist made him want to run and hide in a corner like a child.

"The newspaper office will be the best option for us," Joseph was saying. "If we're lucky we'll find the very writer who produced the clipping. If Patrick Carrigan is still in this vicinity, he'll know. In theory, Liam, we could be reunited with our uncle as early as tomorrow."

"That's being mighty optimistic."

"And why not be optimistic, eh?"

"Because nothing ever goes right for us. You never noticed that?"

"Nonsense! We've had our runs of bad luck, no doubt about it. But destiny is at work here, Liam. A divine hand is guiding us. What would the odds have been of that particular clipping being inside a trunk that we, of all people, just happened to find at a time we were in Kansas? What are the odds that—"

"You've been through all that ten dozen times, Joseph. For mercy's sake, don't do it again."

They rode on, Joseph talking and Liam half listening. It was necessary at times to be at least partially deaf to Joseph the Dreamer's monologues. Otherwise the effect was that of locoweed on cattle. Joseph going full steam could grind a man's mind down to a nubbin, like a relentless dentist filing away a tooth.

Liam shuddered at the thought, reached up, and lightly touched his left jaw, wincing. Maybe the toothache would go away on its own. Or he could get some whiskey and swish it around in his mouth, which sometimes helped. Liam liked that idea. He'd go into Dodge tonight and get himself some whiskey for that bad tooth.

They traveled over a slight swell in the land, and suddenly there it was in the distance: Dodge City, Kansas. They reined their horses to a halt for a moment and looked it over. Not much to see, but Joseph smiled as though it were a vision of paradise. For his part, Liam grunted in acknowledgment of their arrival, hopped down from the saddle, walked away a few paces to urinate, then mounted up again.

"Already marking off your territory?" Joseph said.

"Just needed to piss, that's all. I wonder what kind of hotels they have in Dodge . . . or do you figure we'll have to settle for some hole in the wall?"

"I've got hopes we can avoid both. We can't justify the cost of a hotel, and flophouses give you lice. If all this is meant to be, like I think it is, I believe some other option will present itself."

"Mother Nature's hotel, huh?"

"Probably. Or maybe we can find some old abandoned place and squat there. Or scrounge up enough to buy a cheap tent and pitch it somewhere where it won't be in anybody's way."

A few minutes later, nearer Dodge, Liam pointed out the burned-out remains of a small house on what appeared to be abandoned property. The real attention-getter, however, was the empty barn standing a couple of hundred feet from the house.

"Looks like a free hotel to me," Joseph said.

"Yep. But Lordy, I'll miss that hotel bed. My back is still sore. And sleeping on the ground last night just made it worse."

They entered the barn and found it acceptable. The loft contained enough hay to make beds, and the roof appeared likely to shed water. The stalls below would be ideal for their horses.

Dodge City

By then evening was falling. It was suppertime, and the cafés of Dodge City beckoned. They rode on from their newfound home and reached the outskirts of the most rambunctious city in Kansas just as the lights were being fired up in the saloons and dance halls.

Joseph looked around for the Dellworth Apothecary, whose advertisement was on the back of the newspaper clipping. He didn't spot it, but it was getting dark, and such a business wouldn't be open at this hour. He'd find it tomorrow, if it was still here.

They dined on steak, potatoes, biscuits, beans, and corn, washed down with excellent coffee. Dessert was thick-crusted custard pie. The bill was high for men whose finances were so strained, but they reminded each other that they had found free lodging. They could afford at least one good supper and maybe a good breakfast tomorrow morning.

"But tomorrow, when the stores are open, we'll buy some flour, bacon, and such," Joseph said. "It's cheaper if we cook for ourselves."

Liam's reply was a sharp gasp of pain. His hand shot to his jaw and gripped it, and he leaned over his plate.

"That tooth may have to come out, Liam," Joseph said. "It's not going to get better, you know. Maybe tomorrow we can find a dentist."

"I'll be fine."

"Bad teeth bring bad health."

"I told you, I'll be fine. All I need is some clove oil."

The waiter wandered over and offered more coffee, which was gladly accepted. "My brother here has a bad tooth and needs to find an apothecary for clove oil," Joseph said. "Isn't there a Dellworth Apothecary in town?"

The waiter frowned, thinking. "I don't believe so. . . . I think there was at one time, but it's gone now."

"How long gone?"

"I don't know . . . a year, year and a half."

Joseph nodded and reached for his pocket. "Do me a favor, sir, if you will, and glance over this newspaper story for a moment." He handed the waiter the clipping, which he scanned.

"There's a name in there: Patrick Carrigan, a possible relative of ours who we've lost contact with. Does that name mean anything to you?"

"Ain't heard of him, sir."

"So he's not a local man?"

"I don't think so. I'd have probably heard of him if he was. There's lots of people who come to Dodge who ain't local, though. He was probably just passing through."

Joseph took back the clipping and thanked the waiter. This was disappointing news. If Patrick Carrigan was not a local, the odds of picking up his trail were greatly diminished.

They walked the streets of Dodge when they'd finished their meal, and gave in to the temptation to stop in at a saloon. It was Liam's temptation, really, Joseph being a near teetotaler. Liam had whiskey, Joseph water. Liam claimed the whiskey was for his tooth mostly, and this time Joseph believed it because he could tell his brother truly was in pain. But he also knew that Liam would have found some other reason to drink, even if the tooth weren't bad.

"Think I'll head back," Joseph said at length.

"Can't wait for an evening in a barn, huh? Come on, Joseph, have a beer at least. I swear, folks probably think you're a Baptist preacher, the way you shun alcohol."

"As a good Catholic, I take offense at that."

"A *good* Catholic?"

"I try to be. What about you? How long since you've been to confession, Liam? How long since you've attended Mass?"

"I'm a good little boy. I've got no sins to confess."

Joseph rose to go. "Someday, brother, maybe you'll take life seriously enough."

"You take everything seriously, and look where it's gotten you. You take things seriously and I don't . . . but we're both broke."

"The rain falls on the just and the unjust alike."

"Yes . . . so if the unjust are having more fun, who has the better end of the bargain?"

"Good evening, Liam. Don't get so drunk you can't find your way back to the barn. And don't spend all our money on liquor. I mean it."

"*Our* money? My portion is *my* portion. Don't tell me what to spend it on."

"Fine. And when your portion is gone, don't come begging to me for part of mine."

They stared at one another, anger flaring unexpectedly. It was this way with them, too often, and both regretted it, for each liked the other and would prefer to live without the tension that sometimes dominated their relationship. The tension was worse since the failed cattle drive. A mutual realization passed in silence between them as they glared at each other:

These were hard and uncertain days, a greater strain on them, perhaps, than either had realized.

"I'll see you when you get in," Joseph said quietly, and began to leave. "Be careful, Liam. And I hope your tooth stops hurting."

He mounted his horse and rode quietly through the cattle town, listening to the music and laughter from the saloons. Sounds of celebration, cowboys at the end of a thousand-mile trail, freshly paid, freshly shaved, clipped, and bathed. New clothes, new hats, and an opportunity to celebrate with their meager earnings.

He envied them. To them a little was a lot. But he and Liam had set their stakes much higher. They had counted on their cattle drive to make them a substantial amount of money. For them there was nothing to celebrate in how it had all turned out. The Chisholm Trail had broken them, mile after grueling mile.

Joseph turned his horse and headed back out of town. As he rode back through the thickening Kansas night, a sense of hopelessness overwhelmed him. He wondered how big a failure and fool he really was: a failure because of the botched cattle drive, and a fool because of this probably pointless quest to find an uncle whom both of them had until now written off as gone or even dead. At this moment Joseph clearly saw and despised his own tendency toward self-delusion. One talk with a priest, a few coincidences glued together by his own willingness to find mystical meaning in random events, and he was leading Liam off to discover their "destiny" by tracking down an uncle who perhaps couldn't care less about them even if they did find him.

Joseph was exhausted on all levels when he reached the barn. He dealt with his horse, took his bedding, and headed for the loft.

The hay was soft and warm, the wind oddly soothing as it whispered around the barn. Joseph's mood improved somewhat. He'd feel better after a few hours of sleep. This was Joseph's solution to problems, his escape. Sleep. Letting problems disappear into the back of his mind, to be sorted out in dreams and the workings of the mind that go on even in unconsciousness.

With a final thought about Liam back there in Dodge, and a quick prayer that he'd keep sober and out of trouble, Joseph rolled over in his blankets, settled himself on the hay, and closed his eyes.

6

Liam took another swig of light amber whiskey and swished it around in his mouth, letting the alcohol purify and soothe the aching tooth. It was working pretty well. The tooth didn't hurt so much; it actually felt a little numb now.

He grinned and swallowed the whiskey. The truth was, he was feeling a little numb all over at this point.

He was hungry, too, but a remedy for that was right at hand. On the table before him was a wide-mouthed jar filled with little hard sticks of bread for customers to nibble with their beer. Liam fetched one out, bit into it, chewed—and yelped with pain as a jagged crumb hit the bad tooth and assaulted the tender nerve.

"Honey, what's the matter?"

Liam looked up at the tired-looking but pretty woman who had just cooed so tenderly at him. Just another soiled dove in another saloon, but she had a kind face and appealing smile. "Bad tooth," he said.

She pulled back a chair and sat down beside him. "Oh, honey, I know how that can be. I do despise a toothache. You know what works to ease the pain, don't you?"

"Clove oil."

"Oh, what I'm thinking of is much better than that. Opium."

"Never used it."

"It's marvelous: Just press some into the bad part of the tooth, and you'll not feel it anymore. Not at all. It's a wonderful thing, opium."

"You have some?"

"Back at my place."

Liam took another swig of whiskey, swished it over the tooth, and swallowed. "I think I'd like to try some."

"Well, come on, then, sweetheart. I'll fix you right up. I'll have you feeling just fine before you know it."

Liam stood. The tooth throbbed. He wavered, only just then realizing how much he'd been drinking. He grinned dully at the woman, then accepted her offer of an extended arm. Letting her help support him, he left the saloon with her. She maneuvered him to the right.

Two buildings down, she steered him into an alley. "Here's a fresh fish," she said into the darkness. Two men emerged from the shadows like phantoms. Liam looked at them uncomprehendingly; then one of them struck him in the stomach and the second followed up with a well-placed blow to the jaw that sent a pain such as he'd never known before exploding from the vicinity of the bad tooth and rippling all through his being. He shuddered and collapsed as blood spilled over his lower lip. A second blow to the jaw knocked him over completely.

He was senseless as the woman cleaned out his pockets, then vanished along with the two men into the Kansas night.

Joseph sat up, stared at the barn wall in front of him, and took a moment to comprehend just where he was. As his mind began working again, the pieces fell into place, and he looked over to see if Liam was awake.

Liam was not even there.

Joseph stood, throwing aside his blankets. "Liam?" No reply. He called again, with the same result: Liam was nowhere in the barn.

He shook his head, disgusted but not surprised. Liam had done this kind of thing before. Most likely he was safe and sound somewhere, probably still sleeping off a drunk or suffering from its aftereffects, but you never knew. He could be jailed. He could have let his temper get him into a row and wound up hurt and hospitalized. He could be dead.

Swearing softly beneath his breath, Joseph left the barn and went to the little creek that ran nearby. He stripped off his clothes, took a cold bath right in the creek, then washed out his garments, wrung out all the water he could, and put them all on again still wet. They would dry by the time he reached Dodge.

He was too worried about Liam to think about breakfast. He was angry too: He might have to search for Liam for hours, and if it proved to be only because he'd gotten himself drunk or in trouble, Joseph would be inclined toward homicide.

When he reached Dodge, Joseph realized just how hard this might be. Liam could be literally anywhere. He could be drunk in a back alley, in some cheap dive, or in the room of a soiled dove. He might be in jail . . . or in the undertaker's parlor.

Joseph pondered finding a lawman and inquiring, but decided to try his luck with a blind search first. No point in stirring things up too much to begin with.

He investigated the saloons that stayed open around the clock, hoping to find Liam sleeping one off in a corner. No luck. He inquired of barkeeps about whether they'd seen a man of Liam's description, but the shifts had changed and no one working the saloons that morning had been around the night before to see anyone.

Joseph visited the dance halls next but found them closed. Random inquiries along the street produced no results. He was about ready to go to the law after all when by chance he turned, looked down an alley, and saw a familiar figure rising haltingly and with difficulty, as if he'd been glued to the ground and was fighting the adhesion.

Joseph was at his side in a moment. "Liam! What happened? Are you hurt?"

Liam, whose face was covered in dried blood, collapsed to the ground again, and Joseph nearly panicked. He headed up to the street to shout for help, but Liam said, "No! No . . . I'm all right . . . I think." He sat up, shifting around to get firmly onto his rump. He leaned back against a brick wall. His voice sounded oddly muffled, and he began to spit saliva mixed with old blood. And something else: a tooth.

"I don't think I need to go to the dentist now," Liam said.

"That's the bad tooth?"

"Yes."

"What the devil happened here, Liam?"

"Let me think. . . . It's hard to remember." He frowned blankly a few moments, which gave his handsome face a rather stupid quality. Then he nodded. "I remember. I left the saloon with a woman who was going to give me some clove oil for the tooth."

"A woman. . . . Are you saying a woman did this to you?"

"No. There were men waiting in the alley." He paused and slapped around on his person. "My money's gone, Joseph."

Joseph shook his head. "In Abilene you get stabbed

with a hairpin because you went to a dance hall. Then you get thrown out a second-floor window because you were fool enough to go home with a woman. . . ."

"Bread and jam. That's all it was. Are we in Abilene now?"

Joseph recognized in Liam's addled state the signs of concussion: He needed medical attention.

"No, we're in Dodge, where you've gotten yourself assaulted in an alley because some woman offered you clove oil. Now you're injured, not to mention destitute. What am I supposed to make of you, Liam?"

"Did you say something about bread and jam? I'm hungry."

"No, *you* did. You've probably got a crack in your skull. You look like hell itself. Let's find a doctor. Maybe we can afford one, since we don't have to worry about a dentist bill anymore."

"I hate dentists. Dentists come from hell."

"Forget dentists; it's a physician you need."

"I don't need a physician. I'm fine. We need to get on to Dodge."

"We're *in* Dodge, and you *do* need a physician."

"I'm just dizzy."

"We're taking you to a physician. You're lucky to be alive and lucky I found you."

7

Liam was indeed lucky. The physician who examined him confirmed that he was likely suffering from concussion, but nothing that should do lasting damage—if Liam would take care of himself a few days. As for the blows Liam had received, they'd done no more than bruise him up. The loss of the tooth was actually a benefit, since it had needed pulling anyway.

Even so, a concussion was a concussion, and Liam was ordered to spend two days in complete inactivity, preferably resting in bed. And not a blanket in a hayloft, the doctor said after learning where they were living: a real bed, in real shelter.

Joseph paid the doctor and looked sadly at his dwindling resources. "I'm going to stay in the barn, no matter what he says," Liam stated. "We can't afford a room."

"We can't now . . . but we will be able to after I find a job."

"Look, I don't want to be taken care of like some child or a kept woman. And what if you can't find anything?"

"There's always work, Liam. I can make enough to keep us up here for a while. Something better will come along in good time. And the only reason you'd be kept is for you to recover. A special circumstance."

Liam did not like the idea but gave in for lack of any other real options.

They sought out a cheap boardinghouse, discovered that the owner was Irish, used that as leverage to haggle for an even cheaper price, and put Liam up in real shelter. Joseph, however, remained homeless: The cost of boarding two in the room was beyond their means. Liam would reside alone for the moment; Joseph would remain in the barn outside of town.

"Here," he said to Liam, handing him half of all the money he had in the world. "Just in case you need it and I'm not close by."

"What about you? You may need it more than I do."

"I'll be making more money when I find a job. Don't worry about me. All I ask is that you don't take that money and go out gambling or drinking with it. Please, promise me you won't. Promise me you'll do nothing but rest, like the doctor said."

"I don't make promises. Having to make a promise implies you don't trust me to begin with."

"I want you to swear—on our mother's grave."

"That's sacrilegious, Joseph. I'd never swear on such a sacred thing."

"You'll behave yourself, though, right?"

"I don't make promises, Joseph. I ain't a child no more who has to be told what to do. But yes, I'll behave myself." He privately added, *By my definition, not necessarily yours.*

Joseph turned away, his expression dark. "Well, you sure do act like a child plenty enough. Good-bye. I'm going now."

"I don't need nobody to sweep floors," the man behind the desk said, looking at Joseph across a sea of disorderly papers, heaped instead of stacked. They were in a tiny office off the back of one of Dodge's many saloons.

"No offense, sir," Joseph replied, "but when I walked across your floor just now, there were crunches enough to make me think I was crushing walnuts."

"This here is a saloon. Ain't nobody cares if the floor is clean. A little grit is good: absorbs the tobacco spit."

"I see. Is there anything else you might need? Someone to wash dishes, do general work . . . whatever you may require."

"Listen, mister, you seem a smart enough man. What are you doing looking for such low work as floor sweeping and dishwashing?"

"I'm in a pressing situation, sir. My brother has gotten hurt and has to be laid up in a boardinghouse a few days. I'm looking for a job for the short term to generate enough money to cover his costs."

"What about yours?"

"I don't have many costs. I'm cooking most of my own food and living in an abandoned barn outside of town."

"Abandoned barn? The Arment place?"

"I don't know. There's a burned-out house nearby."

"Oh, yeah, I know the place. That is Ben Arment's old dwelling. It burned down about a year ago, just after Ben left town. But his brother is still about. That's Caleb. Over at the livery."

None of this was of interest to a man who needed only work, not anecdotes. "So, Mr. Smith, there's nothing for me here, then."

"Not here. I hope you find better luck elsewhere. How badly hurt is your brother?"

"Nothing lasting. A few days of rest. Knowing him, he'll not have the patience for it for very long."

Back outside, Joseph paused and looked up and down the street. He'd stopped in three shops and four saloons so far, with no better luck than he'd just had with Smith. He was momentarily tired of job searching, and hungry, so he headed for the cheapest-looking café he could find and ordered salt pork and beans.

As he ate he examined the town through the window and noted the roof of a barnlike structure visible beyond the facade across the street from him. The livery, probably. What name had Smith called? Arment . . . Caleb Arment. Joseph decided to pay a call on him. Maybe Arment needed a hand, and Joseph was good with horses.

It was destiny, as sure as the world. When Joseph reached the livery, a stoutly built man, bald except for a thick fringe of white-gray hair around the ears and the back of the head, was tacking up a sign on the wall: HELP WANTED. Another man, hardly more than a boy and with a generally unsavory look about him, was stalking off up the street, occasionally turning and glaring back at the bald man and making obscene gestures, which the man utterly ignored.

"Mr. Arment, I presume?"

The man turned and eyed Joseph. "I'm Arment. What can I do for you?"

"The name's Carrigan. Joseph Carrigan. I'm here to ask if work might be available."

Arment flicked his eyes toward the sign he'd just hung. "You can see that it is. Ain't much of a job, though. Just general livery work—dirty, smelly, and poor paying. The folks who seem to do work like that generally aren't the sort I can keep around for long, like the boy heading up the street there. I caught him stealing from the till and sent him on his way."

"You'd have no trouble of that sort from me," Joseph replied. He quickly outlined his situation and his request, and Arment's initially cautious expression relaxed. Joseph knew he had a job even before Arment said the words.

They talked pay, which was indeed low but sufficient for Joseph's limited needs. He would start immediately.

Having found help literally minutes after having fired his previous employee put Arment in a good mood, and having a paying job again did the same for Joseph. He began working with a nearly boyish enthusiasm. Arment observed, smiled, and went about his own business.

There was no loss of pride on Joseph's part, moving from the status of cattleman with a herd of his own down to stall cleaner and general assistant in a livery stable. His experiences on the cattle drive had broken him of pridefulness, of which he had never possessed much anyway. His father, who had carried a disdain for the leisure class bordering on scornful, had instilled in both him and Liam the value and dignity of work. Joseph sometimes found that he shared their father's feelings about the idle rich. He suspected that he and Liam might differ on that, however: If Liam had the opportunity to become a wealthy man of leisure, Joseph had no doubt he would leap at the chance.

After work that evening he went to Liam's boardinghouse, bearing sandwiches in a sack. Liam was terribly restless, an unhappy man who felt like an invalid and was ready to defy the physician and get back to a normal life. The only problem was that he was struck by dizziness when he moved around much, had a perpetual headache, and (Joseph noticed without comment) repeated himself frequently.

Liam brightened considerably when he learned of Joseph's job. "It will pay enough to keep us from worrying about food and shelter and so on," Joseph said. "So relax. Don't worry about the cost of this room: I can take care of it."

"Then come move in too. Or get a room of your own if you want."

"No. Covering two is a little harder than covering one. I'm content to stay where I am."

"I'll not stay in a room with a bed while you sleep in a barn."

"Sure you will! You've got cause to be here; I don't. I've slept in much worse than that loft."

Liam didn't argue long. He seemed weary and asked Joseph if he'd bring him some whiskey to help pass the time.

"Whiskey and knocks to the head don't mix, I've heard," Joseph said. "Stay away from it until your noggin is healed."

Liam snorted disdainfully and looked away. "A man don't need a mother when you're around, that's for certain!"

"And he doesn't need a child if he's got you. Be patient, Liam: You took a hard knock."

Joseph departed and headed for the barn. His work at the livery had tired him, and his full and satisfied stomach promised him a good night's sleep. He rode out of Dodge City whistling, greeting people he passed, touching his hat when he happened upon a lady.

He nodded a greeting toward a man who stood in an alleyway, far enough back in the shadows so that little of him could be made out. Joseph could not see, and did not care, whether the man waved back. He was in a good enough humor to be friendly to the jovial and rude alike.

After Joseph had ridden past, the man in the alley emerged from the shadows and out onto the street, where he glowered at Joseph's back as he rode on into the darkness. The man pulled a flask from his pocket, uncorked it, and took a swig, splashing whiskey across his lips and down his chin. He stuck out his tongue to dab at the spillage running through his dirty whiskers, then muttered an obscenity into the night in the direction Joseph had gone.

"Where there's one, there's the other," he murmured in a gravelly voice. "I'll be keeping an eye out for you, Liam Carrigan. That I will."

8

Arment greeted Joseph the next morning in the manner of a man accustomed to employees who sometimes just didn't show up. The warmth of his greeting made Joseph feel he'd done Arment a great favor simply by being there.

"You're going to be the best hand I've ever had," Arment said. "I can tell. I'm lucky to have you working for me, Joe."

"Kind words, Mr. Arment."

"So, Joe, what rooming house is it you're staying in?"

"Well, sir, it's actually only my brother staying there, for the sake of cost, and him being the injured one. I'm putting up elsewhere."

"Really! Where is that?"

"I'm staying in a barn on an abandoned farm."

Arment cocked a brow. "With a burned-out house?"

"Yes . . . I'm told that maybe a brother of yours lived there."

"You're staying in that sorry old barn?"

"It's dry and warm and the rats seem friendly enough. They tell me hello, good-bye, all that."

Arment grinned and shook his head. "Ah, me! Staying in that old barn! You be careful there, then."

Joseph was relieved. He'd feared Arment might evict him. As humble an abode as that barn loft was, it was the only one he had, and he couldn't afford to lose it.

The livery was in dire need of painting, and Arment was inspired about mid-morning to launch into that project, now that he had help he could rely on. He gave Joseph a quick lesson on how to run the operation, just in case a customer showed up in his absence, then headed into town with a wagon to buy paint.

By early afternoon both Joseph and Arment were hard at work with brushes and buckets, perched precariously on rickety ladders Arment produced from somewhere in the back of the stables. The rough wood drank paint like a sponge, and Joseph's arms soon ached. Although Arment had bought a lot of paint, it appeared likely he'd have to go back for more before this thirsty building would be covered.

They were taking a needed break around three o'clock when a ramshackle wagon pulled by a scrawny mule came rolling by. On the driver's seat sat a tired-looking, drawn woman in a blue linsey-woolsey skirt that was threadbare but neat. She might have been pretty once, but now had the drained and dried-out appearance common to so many frontier women. There were two wiry little boys, raggedly dressed but clean and combed, riding in the rear of the wagon, their eyes darting back and forth, taking in the town with such eagerness that Joseph guessed they didn't get to come there often.

The family wore their poverty like a shroud, though the cleanliness of their clothing gave Joseph the impression that they tried hard to hide it. However, there was one thing about them that made them stand out distinctly: The man driving the wagon wore a mask of sorts, made from the cloth of a flour sack. It was tied around the left side of his face, completely covering that side of his head, including his eye. The mask was filled out completely, but it had a lumpiness about it that made it appear partially stuffed with old rags or some other such filler. The man's one visible eye flashed toward Arment and Joseph as the family rode by; the man's head dipped subtly and quickly in greeting. Arment raised a hand and Joseph nodded back.

"There's a pitiful thing for you," Arment said after they were on down the street. "What a horrible thing war is!"

Joseph mulled that for a moment and understood. "He wears the mask to cover a war injury?"

"Yes. I assume it was the war, anyway. I don't know what else could do such damage to a man. Amazing that he's alive."

"Have you seen under the mask?"

"No, but those who have say it's a horrible thing. Much of his face, even part of his head, is just gone. No eye in the socket, either. How he lived through such an injury is beyond my ken."

"Where do they live?"

"West of town, out some miles. In a sod house, I think. They have that look of sod-house dwellers . . . a kind of dirtiness that gets into the skin, into the very essence of a person, and that you can't get out again no matter how hard you try."

"Their clothes were clean, anyway," Joseph said, pitying this unknown family and feeling oddly obligated to say something kind about them, as if he were their apologist.

"Yes. The poor mother tries hard, I suppose. But what a life! Living with a husband who is mangled and so ashamed he hardly comes to town . . . having nothing but dirt around you, nothing but rags to wear. Sad. Sad indeed."

"What's their name?"

"Scott, I think. I don't know first names."

Joseph watched the wagon, far down the street now

and preparing to make a turn. He saw three young boys playing on the boardwalk stop and stare. One of them shouted something Joseph could not make out, and another stooped to pick up a stone. He acted as if he would throw it at the man in the mask, but apparently lost his courage.

"See that?" Arment said.

"Yes."

"It's how they are treated here. Scott barely comes into town because of it. People treat the poor man as if he is evil, just because he scares them. A sorry breed, the human race! God forgive us for being like we are, eh? God forgive us."

They went back to their painting, moods somewhat subdued. In the back of Joseph's mind played scenes he wished he could forget, horrors he had observed on battlefields when he had worn a blue uniform and wondered in every battle if one of the gray-clad phantoms he shot at was his own brother.

He'd seen men mangled terribly. The worst cases, thankfully, usually received the mercy of death from their injuries. But a few, like this Scott, survived to carry with them eternal reminders of war.

Joseph painted, mulling the fact that despite all the ill fortune he and Liam had endured, they were really both quite lucky men. They had come through war alive and unmangled. They had health and wits, and lived in a nation that allowed the free exercise of both toward the end of one's own advancement. And children did not shout at them or throw rocks when they passed.

They were lucky indeed.

But maybe not Liam, Joseph reconsidered. He'd come through unmarred in the physical sense, but his psyche was a different story. There were things he wouldn't talk about, times he would grow grim and moody and lost in something that seemed to haunt him like a ghost. At such times Joseph could look into the eyes of his brother and all but see the war still raging, men still dying, screaming, holding their own severed limbs, crying like terrified children.

But Liam would never talk of it. He would never tell the things he was seeing in his dark moments, nor explain the nightmares that made him bolt upright in his bed, screaming and clawing at his face.

Maybe it was impossible to come through a war truly unmangled. Men like that poor Scott fellow carried their wounds in their flesh, men like Liam in their minds and souls.

Maybe that was why Liam tended to drink and carouse. Maybe it was his way of escaping something that couldn't escape him.

Joseph understood better than he might ever admit to Liam. He himself knew what it was to be haunted. In Joseph's case, the haunting had driven him, not to liquor and women, but more deeply to the Catholic faith his good Irish father had raised him in. In his faith he could sometimes make a kind of sense out of things that seemed nonsensical.

And he could deal with the guilt that rose every time he remembered the woman, and the baby, and—

He shut off the thought and painted as though his life depended upon it.

9

Arment raised Joseph's pay the next day—a token amount, but enough to make a difference, and a point. He handed Joseph his first wages, more than Joseph had expected, and explained about the raise.

Joseph accepted appreciatively. He liked Arment, and he liked the livery business, grubby and malodorous as it was. Already his scheming and dreaming side had him and Liam opening livery stables in towns like this across the advancing West. Carrigan Brothers Livery, they could call it. Or, to avoid the Irish stigma, maybe J & L Stables. They would sell feeds, too, and tack gear, saddles, and the like. In the bigger cities they would hire horse doctors to affiliate with them. Their stables would emphasize cleanliness. The employees would wear specially designed white jackets. When one got dirty, they would replace it with a clean one. They'd hire some skilled Chinese to keep up with all the laundry.

A nice idea. But getting the money on the front end to launch such a venture was daunting. Joseph would have to scheme and dream a long time to figure out that one.

Joseph took his lunch late by choice. He ate a sandwich while walking across town, looking for an address he'd scrawled on a scrap of paper. To his good fortune, the editor was in and in a cooperative good humor. A pressman was busily printing the latest edition, full of typical Dodge City rough-and-ready journalism.

The editor leaned back in his chair and rubbed his chin. "Carrigan. Patrick Carrigan . . . Yes, I remember the name. I recall that story. Quite a little row that was. Two tables broken, and one chair, if memory serves."

"My interest is in finding whether this Patrick Carrigan might be living around here."

"He does not, to my knowledge. I recall him as a cattleman traveling through. I have no idea where he was from or where he was going."

"Do you remember what he looked like?"

"I caught only a glimpse of him myself, when he was coming into court and I happened to be walking out. I didn't write that story; a man who worked for me did it, but he's gone—moved to Wichita to take a job there, and I hear has moved on since to somewhere else. You could ask the judge or the bailiff. But both see so many cases that I doubt you'd get much information."

"There would be an address on file in the court records, though, wouldn't there?"

"I presume so. But these cattlemen passing through give all kinds of addresses, usually some town back east that they haven't been back to for years. Some of them don't really have an address, other than whatever cattle trail they happen to be following or whatever ranch they work for."

Joseph thanked the editor and left, wondering if he had time to venture to the courthouse. Deciding that Arment would be forgiving if he was a little late, he did go to the courthouse, but found nothing to help him. The records for the period that Patrick Carrigan had appeared in court had been stored temporarily in a shed behind the courthouse, and the shed had caught fire in a lightning storm. No records: no way to see what address Patrick Carrigan had given.

Joseph headed back to the livery and apologized for his lateness. As he had anticipated, Arment was forgiving. He inquired about Joseph's luck.

"It was bad. Nothing substantial from the newspaper, and the court records for that period were accidentally destroyed."

"This uncle of yours is going to be hard to track, it seems."

"Maybe it isn't even my uncle. There's bound to be more than one Patrick Carrigan in the world. Maybe I should just give up looking for him. He may be dead, for all I know."

Liam sliced off a big piece of salt pork and shoved it into his mouth, following it up with a chunk of biscuit. Joseph, eating more slowly, observed his brother's voraciousness with amusement. They were in Liam's rented room, eating food that Joseph had brought up from a café.

"I believe you're hungry, Liam."

"Starved. You sit around all day, going loco, staring at the walls, and all you can think about is food. And beer. And women. And getting to walk around free like a man should."

"I know it's hard to be laid up, Liam, but you're doing it for your health. A busted head is nothing to take lightly."

"My head ain't busted, Joseph. I took a knock, that's all, no worse than I've had plenty of times before, and now I feel fine. It's crazy for me to be staying here like this. I might as well be in a jail cell."

"Be patient for a day or two more, Liam. You'll be in the clear before long, and then you can find a job."

"Find a job, huh? So we're settling in Dodge awhile?"

"I think it makes sense for us to build up some money."

"Did you get to the newspaper to ask about that clipping?"

"Yes." Joseph related what had happened and told about the destroyed court records as well.

"So the trail is cold," Liam noted.

"For now, yes. But I intend to keep asking. I'm going to talk to Arment about it and see if he knows a Patrick Carrigan. It's even possible that there might be some record of him using the livery, if he was just traveling through."

"Does Arment keep many detailed records about people who use the stable?"

"Well, no. I don't think so. But maybe he'll remember something."

"Should we even be wasting our time looking for Patrick at all?"

"It's not wasting our time. I still think that clipping came into my possession for a reason. We're supposed to find him."

"Destiny, right?"

"I believe so."

Liam shook his head. "Everything's that way with you, brother. Always some unseen design, or destiny, or whatever you call it."

Joseph smiled. "Faith is the evidence of things not seen."

"Whatever you say."

They ate the last of their meal in silence, then Joseph said, "I'm not going to be living in that barn much longer. And maybe, just maybe, you won't be living here."

"How so?"

"When I was leaving today, Arment told me he's going to fix up a room in the loft of the livery stable. It's just storage right now, but it's good and tight, and with some wood put up to line it, and an old rug thrown down on the floor, it would make a good enough place for a man to stay. We're working on the room tomorrow, and I'll move in tomorrow night."

"How much is he charging you?"

"Nothing. That's the good thing about it. Since I'll be there most all the time, the place will be more secure. The room serves in lieu of pay for making the place a little safer. And I'm going to tell him about you and see if maybe he'll let you move in too. Two guards are better than one, right?"

"Would he pay me?"

"I don't know. . . . Even if he doesn't, free lodging is a kind of pay. You could get your own job during the days and help me guard the place at night—assuming Arment will go along with it."

"It would be a hell of a secure livery, huh? Two night guards."

"Yep. Arment ought to like that, though."

Liam was thinking that he had no intention of being tied to some closed livery at night—not after he got work and had a jingle in his pocket. Night was the time for drinking and dancing. And what about women? How could he bring a woman back to his dwelling with Joseph there, grinning his stupid grin and talking about faith and destiny and such? He kept all this to himself, however.

"So you're in with this fellow for the long term, it would seem."

"For a while, anyway. But look, Liam, it makes sense: It's a place to stay, and a paying job. Speaking of which—" he pulled from his pocket the pay he had received that morning, and doled half of it out to Liam—"there you go. See? We're getting better off already because I've got that job."

"So we are. It paid for supper, right? Hey, who's going to take these dishes back to the café?"

"I'll do it."

"I don't mind it. I'd like the chance to get out." He glanced at the money in his hand. "I ought to do something. . . . I feel like a charity case right now."

"Don't worry about it. Pay me back after you get a job, if you want. If you don't, it doesn't matter. And I'll take the dishes back. Want me to find you something to read to pass the time? I can bring you a book on my way to work in the morning."

"Do that. I like *Gulliver's Travels*. You read that? It was Daniel Boone's favorite book, you know. You've heard of him, I suppose."

"I have. Kind of like you: He hated to stay put."

"I'm not staying in this room beyond tonight, Joseph. Cracked skull or not, I'm getting out of here and back to living again. I hate this being cooped up. I might even take a walk tonight."

"It makes you dizzy just to walk around the room. I don't think you should push yourself."

"I'm just sick of being a prisoner."

"It's not been that long. But I don't blame you: I'd hate it too. Just be patient. Patience is a virtue."

"You know me and virtue. We just ain't that comfortable with one another."

From the shadows across the street, two men watched Joseph leave Liam's room. They'd seen him earlier, carrying two trays of food, and had followed him. Now he carried out both trays empty.

"Maybe he's got a woman he keeps in there," one suggested.

The other shook his head. "No. Not him. He's a high-and-mighty holy type, not the kind to keep a whore girl. His brother's in there, sure as hell."

"Why would he have to carry food to his brother?"

"Don't know. Maybe he's laid up sick or hurt."

"So what do you want to do?"

"Don't know yet." He raised a bottle and swallowed a big mouthful of whiskey. "I want to think this one through. This is too fine an opportunity to waste. I'm going to make Liam Carrigan pay for shaming me like he did before all them men." He took another swig.

"Hell, Mack, you can't blame him much, can you? You tried to shoot him!"

"He deserved it."

"You were going to back-shoot him, though. You said so yourself. Ain't nobody deserves to be back-shot."

"Since when did you get religion?"

"It ain't that. It just ain't right to back-shoot somebody."

"I ain't spent a moment of my life worrying about what's right, except what's right for me. Hell, if he's laid up over there in bed or something, I ought to just go over and put a slug in him with nobody around to see."

"Not with me here you won't. I'll not be a witness to murder, Mack."

Mack opened his mouth to reply, but at that moment the door across the street opened and Liam Carrigan emerged. He looked about and from side to side, as if checking to make sure the way was clear, then turned and walked down the street, hands in his pockets. His pace quickened as he went on, and they heard him start to whistle.

"If he was laid up, he sure ain't now," Mack said. "Come on. Let's follow him."

"Not me, Mack. I'll not be drawed into no killing."

"Suit yourself, then."

Mack waited for Liam to get a little farther away, then stepped out of the shadows, crossed the street, and followed in Liam's track.

10

Just a walk. That's all he'd planned it to be. Just a short, easy stroll up and down the street. Get his bearings and equilibrium back. Stretch his legs.

The short walk had become a long one, winding around the streets and alleys of Dodge. Rather than feeling more dizzy, he felt better the farther he went. His headache was even diminishing.

Hang physicians, and hang Joseph. Liam's instinct all along had been that he could shake this thing off more quickly by keeping moving than just lying around. He'd made the right choice in taking this walk.

Now, though, he was facing a strong temptation to make a wrong choice. The saloon before him was bright and cheerful and inviting. He heard music and laughter and the clink of bottle necks on shot glasses, and the whirring of a gambling wheel. He heard a woman's voice, bright and pretty to hear, saying something he couldn't make out, then laughing.

Liam wanted to be in that saloon in the worst way.

He swore beneath his breath. The money in his pocket had been given him by Joseph. He didn't have the right to spend it in a saloon.

Or did he? Joseph had said he could pay him back later on. Which would make this his money, not Joseph's.

All he needed was one drink, maybe two. No cards, no women. Just a drink or two. And he could ask around about work, maybe actually find a job in one of the all-night entertainment establishments that teemed in Dodge. He could inquire with people about whether they knew anyone named Patrick Carrigan. Nothing to feel guilty about.

The guilt was there nonetheless when he walked through the door. He reminded himself that he'd pay Joseph back as soon as he had work of his own. What he would spend tonight, which wouldn't be much, was rightly his to spend.

He found a table and sat down, so glad to be in a saloon again that he couldn't help but grin.

One of the guiding rules that Joseph's father had drilled into him was one that had proven itself to Joseph many times: "Son," the old man had said, "when instinct tells you there is danger, always, always heed it."

So when Joseph heard the slow cacophony of hoofbeats approaching him from the darkness ahead, and an alarm sounded in some recess of his brain, he didn't doubt himself for a moment. He turned off the road and headed into a little clump of cottonwoods growing beside a creek and from his hiding place watched as a half-dozen horsemen rode by. The moon had been friendly, ducking behind a fast-moving cloud as he left the road but coming out again as the riders went by. He was able to see them clearly, although he was unobserved himself.

They were all big men, all bearded, and all well armed. Joseph noted the butts of rifles in saddle boots, and the pistols holstered on each man. He heard one man talking, his voice low and gruff. Joseph couldn't make out exactly what he said beyond a few cusswords.

He waited until the group was past before he emerged and rode on toward the barn that was, for one more night, the closest thing he had to a home. He was glad he'd avoided the riders. The notion that they would not have let him pass without trouble couldn't be shaken.

Joseph held the lighted match aloft until it burned down to his fingers, when he was forced to shake it out. Then he lighted another and gaped again at the scattered mess that had once been his few possessions.

Several items were gone, his two extra shirts and

pairs of trousers among them. His shaving gear was still there, but his socks were gone, and his two extra handkerchiefs. A paring knife was missing, along with all of his stored food. No skillet. His coffee tin was gone and his coffeepot had been stomped flat, probably in pure meanness. The Dutch oven was gone, though his metal plate and three-pronged fork remained.

Worst of all, his Colt pistol with the bone handle, and the bowie knife with the handle that matched it, were gone, along with the gun belt he'd bought in San Antonio a year ago. The pistol and the knife had been gifts from a fellow soldier, a Marylander who had served at Joseph's side nearly through the entire war. Randall Pink, ironically, had survived horrific combat for two years, only to die a year after the war of an infection picked up from a rusted nail he chanced to step upon.

Joseph shook out the second match and sank onto his haunches there in the dark barn loft, feeling sick at heart. He'd not anticipated anything like this. An abandoned barn had seemed a safe enough place to keep his possessions. What thief would come poking around such an unpromising place?

Joseph realized that the thief might still be about. It was dark there; he could be hiding in the loft itself at that moment, mere yards away from him. Joseph lit another match and looked around, then another three in succession as he explored possible hiding places.

Satisfied that whoever had done this was gone, Joseph descended to the ground level, lit an ancient candle stub that was stuck in a holder on the wall, and examined the ground. Fresh hoofmarks—lots of them.

Joseph shook his head. He'd bet that the very riders he'd avoided on the road were responsible for this theft.

He could let go of all of it except the pistol and the bowie. Those mattered to him, and by heaven, he'd get them back if he could.

Joseph mentally cursed the thieves who'd done this. He cursed himself for having been complacent about the safety of his goods. He cursed the gun law in Dodge City that forbade carrying arms, which was the reason he'd opted to leave his pistol behind in the barn in the first place. Why had he not had the foresight to stash it in his saddlebag, or to give it to Arment to keep locked up in his office at the livery stable?

All Joseph could do was pace about and stew bitterly over his loss. He thought about going into Dodge City and tracking down the thieves, but there were six of them and only one of him—assuming the group he'd seen was responsible for this theft at all. It seemed likely, but he'd have trouble proving it.

Even if he did prove it, they'd probably just shoot him down. They looked the type. And he had no pistol now to use either for persuasion or self-defense. He'd sold his Winchester back in Abilene to generate a few extra dollars. Now he was weaponless.

Well, if nothing else, he could ride back into town and tell Liam what had happened: share the misery a little and make himself feel better.

No. It would accomplish nothing. And Liam would get angry and probably head out to track down the thieves himself. He'd get himself hurt—or worse.

Joseph could do nothing but pace about until he was tired of it, then settle down as best he could with no bedroll and try to get some sleep.

Liam, blissfully ignorant of his brother's ill fortune, was in an excellent humor. It was a grand and marvelous thing to be free again, out on the town, enjoying the saloons, the taste of whiskey, the smell of smoke hanging in the air, the feel of cards in his hand.

Somewhere halfway through the second drink, his feeling of guilt had stood up and taken his self-restraint by the hand, and the two of them had walked out of the saloon together, leaving Liam alone at the table.

Good riddance. An evening of cards and drink was just what he needed to feel like himself again.

He eyed his hand and threw a chip into the pile in the center of the table. He had a good feeling about this one. He'd win this hand. . . .

And he did. Luck was on his side tonight. He'd won more than he'd lost—not a common occurrence.

He lost the next two hands, then hit a winning

streak again. Then he did something that made him proud: He stood up and left the game. He'd taken the money Joseph had given him and multiplied it. He was better off than when he'd come in.

Liam felt downright virtuous. He was doing his part to better his situation, and Joseph's.

Time now for a good beer, and maybe one of those cheap cigars they sold out of a jar on the bar top.

He had just sat back down at his table with a cigar in one hand and beer in the other when someone slid up to his side.

"Evening, handsome," the painted woman said. He turned and eyed her but saw nothing to interest him. She was wrinkled and overly perfumed . . . though the perfume failed to mask the woman's bodily odors.

"Evening," he said.

"Mind if I join you? You look lonely sitting at this table."

"Ma'am, the last time I said yes to such a proposition, I wound up in an alley with my skull busted and my money stolen."

"She must have been one strong woman."

"It wasn't her. It was the toughs she had waiting for me out in the alley."

"I've got no toughs out in any alleys. I've got nobody but little old me."

Little was not the right word, but Liam kindly let that pass. "Thanks, but no thanks. I've taken a vow: no sin or vice." *Unless the women are young and pretty,* he added mentally.

"No sin or vice, huh? What about the cards and beer?"

"Virtues, ma'am. The truth is, you're just too much woman for a shy fellow like me."

She winked and blew him a kiss. "If you change your mind . . ."

"I'll keep you in mind."

"I can get you over that shyness."

"I'll bet you can."

Liam finished his beer and started on another. He watched the poker game and thought about entering it again. But no: He was still ahead, spending not the money Joseph had given him but the money he'd won.

He had every right to be there, and felt no need to hurry back to that lonely gray room.

Luck was with him tonight. Nothing could go wrong.

11

The headache was back, vaguely, and Liam wondered just how he'd feel when morning came. At the moment he didn't care. He had as much money in his pocket as when he'd arrived, and he'd enjoyed an evening out of that sorry, dark room.

It had been a legitimate excursion anyway: He had asked about a job at a couple of places along the street. No luck, but he'd asked. And he'd inquired with a barkeep or two about Patrick Carrigan. Again, no luck, but the point at the moment was that he'd tried.

Only a hundred yards away from the saloon, where the street grew darker, he sensed he was being followed—a sensation not totally muted by his slight intoxication whispered to him of danger. A footpad, perhaps, who had seen him win at the poker table and wanted to see just how much money Liam had in his pockets.

Liam walked a little faster, then turned into a dark alleyway. Sure enough, a man walked past moments later, but Liam saw right away it was no footpad, just a drunk weaving his way down the dark street.

Liam let the man get past and stepped onto the street again.

"Sir?"

The voice was soft and very feminine—young, and touched with a vulnerability that one seldom heard from the kind of females who accosted men on dark streets in western Babylons like this one.

Liam turned and saw a young woman approaching him. She was silhouetted against the brighter part of the street behind her so he could make out no features: Only the shapeliness of the silhouette was worthy of note.

"Evening, miss."

"Sir, can you help me?" That same vulnerable-sounding voice, a little tremulous. Yet, as she walked she put a deliberate sway into her hips that didn't imply innocence.

She reached him and stood looking up at his face, visible to her while hers was invisible to him. He had the strongest impression, however, that she was beautiful—a feeling possibly developed after plenty of years in the company of beautiful women, many of them of the same ilk as this young woman . . . assuming she was what he believed she was.

"How can I help you?"

"Well, it's not really me who needs help. It's my sister."

"Sister?"

"Yes. My twin. She's in the alley over there, lying on the ground. I think she's ill."

"Ill?"

The girl laughed. "Do you always repeat the last word people say to you?"

"Do you always laugh while your sister is lying ill in an alley?"

"I don't think she's bad ill. Just a little ill. Maybe there's something that you could do to make her feel better."

He started to tell her that she had the most original solicitation approach he'd yet run across, but he felt a grain of doubt. Might she be telling him the truth?

"How much has your sister had to drink tonight?"

"That's what has me worried, sir: She hasn't touched a drop, but she fell down anyway. Can you come take a look at her?"

"I'm no physician, miss."

"No, but maybe you can help me revive her."

My, but she smelled delightful. Some kind of perfume Liam couldn't identify, as soft and delicate as her voice. That warning instinct of danger began to give way to feelings of a different sort.

But there was no way he'd follow her into a dark alley. Not after what had happened the last time he'd done that.

"Go see if she's up on her own," he said.

"Sir, please . . ." Her voice had a touch of urgency, and she came a half-step nearer to him. "Please. I'm worried about her." She touched his arm, and he noticed she was trembling.

Maybe this was legitimate, not what he suspected.

"Well . . . all right. Let's have a look at her."

"Thank you, sir."

As they turned to head across the street, enough light from the saloons down the way caught her face and gave him his first real look at her, dim though it was. That instinct was right: She was a true beauty. Overly painted, like most in her profession, but still quite pretty. It was impossible to tell her age, but he doubted she was out of her teens.

He followed her into the alley, wary now, thinking again of that back-alley attack the night he'd arrived in Dodge. But nothing happened right away. They simply proceeded down the alley until they came out at the far end, at the rear of the row of buildings.

"I thought you said she was in the alley."

Her arms went around him, caressing, her face suddenly near his, turned upward.

"I think she must have gotten up and gone away on her own."

Liam chuckled. "I should have figured as much."

"I saw you in the saloon," she said. "You're mighty handsome."

"Kind of you to—"

His words were cut off by her lips pressing his. That perfume filled his nostrils and his consciousness. He felt her warm against him, put his arms around her, and returned her kiss with passion.

"Is there a place we can go?" she asked him, reaching up, stroking his cheek with a soft hand.

"Why are you trembling?" he asked.

"I'm not."

"You are. Your whole body is trembling."

She kissed him again, as if to distract him.

Something clicked in his mind. Her mix of innocence and forced, hip-swaying seductiveness, the very odd pretext by which she had lured him, her obvious nervousness . . .

"You're new to this, aren't you."

"Don't talk, handsome. Just kiss me. And take me to your place." She stroked his cheek again but at the same time turned her head and glanced to her right, as if looking for someone or something in the inky blackness, a blackness so thick he could scarcely see her face, as close as she was.

That warning instinct flashed to life again. "Look, miss . . . what's going on here?"

She tensed; her manner changed and suddenly she was speaking in an urgent whisper. "I'm sorry. . . . I didn't want to do it. . . . He gave me money. I think he wants to hurt you!"

"Who?"

A match flared off to the right and touched the end of a cigar clamped in the mouth of a man. The light of the match illuminated a face both familiar and despised.

"Well," Liam said. "Mack Stanley. Who'd have thought we'd run across each other this evening?"

"It was no accident, believe me," Stanley said, tossing down the match.

The girl spoke frantically. "I'm sorry. I'm sorry. I only did it because he gave me money."

"I'm sure there's plenty more you do for money," Liam said, pushing her away.

She turned to Stanley, now virtually invisible again. "What are you going to do to him?"

"Get off with you, Lilly. Your part in this is over."

"You ain't going to kill him, are you?"

"Get out of here, whore!"

"I won't take part in a murder!" Her voice was growing shrill.

Stanley swore bitterly at her, threatening her.

"I'm sorry," she murmured in Liam's direction. Then she was gone like a ghost, backing away into the darkness. But she did not flee, Liam noticed. She lingered back there, just out of sight, watching.

Liam figured the smart thing to do would be to turn and vanish back up the alley, the way he'd come, before Mack could do anything to him. He was unarmed, after all, in compliance with Dodge City's gun laws. He doubted Mack was so law-abiding.

But he would not run. He hadn't run from Mack the time Mack tried to gun him down from hiding on the cattle drive. Instead, Liam had beaten him nearly senseless. He'd rather take a bullet than run from a weasel like Mack.

The cigar flared brightly in the darkness, an inch or two closer than it had been. "Bet you didn't think you'd see me again."

"Never thought about it, Mack."

"I ain't forgot what you done to me. I ain't forgot what it was like to hear all them men laughing at me. I ain't forgot what it was like to lie on the ground at your feet, so beat up I couldn't rise. I ain't forgot a bit of it."

"I didn't intend you to forget it. What surprises me is that you'd come back for more."

"It's different this time, Carrigan." There was the click of a pistol hammer at waist level. "This time I got the advantage."

"This is straight-out murder."

"It don't matter."

"You got a witness. She's still back there."

Mack was silent, briefly. "You, girl . . . get on with you. Get out of here."

"I didn't know you were going to kill him," she said, her voice drifting like a phantom from the darkness.

"Get out of here and you won't know what I do! Get on! I don't need nobody watching this."

She burst into tears. They listened to the sound of her receding footsteps. It came to Liam's mind that he should hate the girl for cooperating with Mack Stanley, but he didn't. She had a sorrowful, frightened-fawn quality that made him pity her.

"Well, now," Mack said. "It appears we're alone. Liam Carrigan, you son of a bitch, get ready to—"

Liam moved up fast and let the glow of the cigar ash guide his fist. It shot out like a cannonball and drove the cigar back into Mack's mouth just before it knocked out his front teeth. Mack made a very strange noise and fell. Liam took a guess, aimed blindly, and kicked hard for what he hoped was Mack's crotch. He got it. Mack let out a grunt that could make a man shudder, and writhed like a worm on the ground.

Liam reached down, felt about, and located the pistol. Mack had dropped it at the same moment he'd lost his teeth. Liam pointed the pistol at him.

"I'm taking this, Mack. May as well take off the gun belt and give it to me too."

Mack whimpered and wept and tried to speak but couldn't around his mouthful of blood and teeth.

"Take off the gun belt or I'll do some more dental work," Liam said.

Mack scrambled; the belt came loose and he tossed it at Liam. It struck Liam in the legs and dropped to the ground. He picked it up, stuck the pistol in the holster, and secured it with the leather string.

"Don't let me see you again, Mack. Not ever. You understand me?"

Mack made weeping noises.

"Talk to me! You understand?"

"Yeth."

"Farewell, Mack. Take care of that mouth when you can."

He turned and walked back up the alley and out into the street. The girl was there, alone and weeping. She seemed very surprised to see Liam, then a smile burst over her face, giving way to a look of fear. Then she saw the gun belt in Liam's hand, turned, and ran away.

Liam had lost his taste for the nightlife of Dodge City. He headed for his room, hiding the gun belt under his canvas coat to avoid trouble. Briefly he wondered if he would have further trouble from Mack. He doubted it. Twice now he'd beaten and humiliated the man. Surely even such a stubborn fool as Mack had enough sense to know when he had bitten off more than he could swallow.

On the other hand, Mack was a back-shooter by nature. And not given to much sense, either.

Liam would watch his back as long as he was in Dodge.

12

Joseph rode into town the next morning, bearing everything he possessed, significantly less than before. He rode to the livery, stabled his horse, and thanked the heavens for the hundredth time that he still had his horse and saddle. A man could lose many things and still get by, but to lose a horse and saddle would be like a kick in the gut.

He told Arment what had happened. Arment was furious. "Six riders, you say? Well, if any such band comes here, I'll call the law in on them."

"I was wondering about that, you know. If they might come in here. Even thieves need livery services, I suppose."

"If they do, we'll do our best to identify them. Would you know them if you saw them?"

"I don't know. The only look I got was from the side of the road, without good light. And I didn't know at the time that I had reason to look closely at them, you know."

"What kind of men were they?"

"Hard cases. Hard-looking men."

"I'll get Marshal Bassett in here if they show up."

"That barn is outside of the city limits, right?"

"Yes."

"Then I'd like to ask if you'd let me run over to the county sheriff's office for a few minutes and report the theft. Maybe they'll spot these scoundrels."

"Go ahead. Take all the time you need."

Joseph found not the sheriff but a bored-looking deputy who took the report with no evidence of caring much about it. Joseph supposed that in a county such as this, where there was enough transient traffic to ensure plenty of thefts and fights and so on, one more report of stolen items didn't amount to much.

The deputy closed out the interview with a question that threw a different light onto the entire matter, anyway.

"That barn you stayed in, was it yours?"

"No. It belongs to my employer, Arment, over at the livery."

"You were there with permission?"

"Well, not at the start, but he's given permission now."

"But your items were just left unguarded in an open barn that wasn't your property and is accessible to anybody."

"Yes, I guess so."

"Ever hear the expression 'finders keepers,' sir?"

Joseph mulled it over, and nodded. He didn't like the deputy's point, but a point it was.

"I suppose I have to resign myself that I've just lost my goods," he said.

"Might be for the best. It would be hard to prove it a true theft. I guess Arment could accuse them of trespassing, but he's not marked the property, and you were a trespasser yourself when you left those goods there."

Joseph nodded again and rose. "Thank you for your time, deputy."

As he was leaving he paused and turned back to the deputy. "Another question, unrelated: Have you ever known a man named Patrick Carrigan in Dodge? Probably would go back two, three years."

The deputy's brows lowered, then he shook his head. "Can't say I have. He a local?"

"No, I don't believe he ever really lived here. He passed through and got into some trouble." Briefly he recounted what the clipping had to say.

"I don't know him. But you might want to ask around some of the local lawyers. If he was in trouble, one of them might have defended him."

It was a good thought, probably the only valuable thing that would come out of this interview. Joseph thanked the deputy, mentally said farewell to his beloved pistol, knife, and other goods, and headed back to the livery.

Along the way he stopped by Liam's room, but found Liam was not there. Out for breakfast, perhaps. It appeared his brother had brought his time of healing rest to an end. No surprise there. Joseph hadn't really expected Liam to hold out as long as he had.

No band of six rough-looking riders ever called at Arment's Livery that day, and as the hours passed and Joseph and Arment lost themselves in their work fixing up the room that would become Joseph's home, the theft at the barn was substantially forgotten.

Joseph was surprised at midday by the arrival of Liam, whom he introduced to Arment.

"Your brother tells me you've been laid up," Arment said.

"Not anymore. I'm back among the living again. Feeling fine. Just dropped by to talk to Joseph a minute—when he's not busy, of course. I'll come back later if need be."

"It's eating time anyway. I'll leave you two to talk. Good to meet you, Liam."

"How's that room coming?" Liam asked Joseph after Arment had wandered down the street toward his favorite café

"It'll be ready before the day's out. No more living in a barn . . . and getting robbed."

"Robbed?"

"That's right." Joseph told his story. "The thing I

hate most is losing the pistol," he concluded. "You know the history behind that pistol. Besides, a man feels sort of helpless without his sidearm."

Liam pinched his lips together, brows knitting. "I'll be back," he said abruptly, and left.

They were back at work, nailing up lumber to panel the interior walls, when Liam showed up again, carrying something in a burlap sack. He called Joseph off to the side, away from Arment, and presented the bag to him.

It contained a Colt pistol, almost identical to the one that had been stolen from Joseph, in a worn but good gun belt. The pistol's handles were maple, worn down and not as pretty or durable as the bone handles on Joseph's lost pistol, but not bad at all.

"I don't understand, Liam. Where did this come from?"

"I came by it last night."

"Last night? I thought you were still laid up last night."

"I couldn't bear it. I had to get out. I went looking for work and asking around for anyone who might have known Patrick Carrigan. No luck on either score."

"How'd you get the pistol?"

"That's an interesting story. That pistol used to belong to Mack Stanley."

"Mack?"

"That's right. I took it from him last night." Liam told his story, leaving out the part about Lilly because he knew Joseph's attitude toward that kind of thing and didn't want to get him going.

"Sounds like we both had an eventful evening," Joseph said. "I'm glad he didn't get the drop on you."

"He'd been better off just to back-shoot me, like he tried to do the first time. But there was that pride aspect, I guess. He wanted me to know it was him."

"I lost a pistol, and you came by one. Things balance out, I guess."

"You don't mind carrying Mack Stanley's pistol?"

"I don't consider it his anymore. He lost right to it when he tried to kill you with it, as far as I'm concerned. Besides, if I have it, he can't use it to shoot you in the back. But he could get another. You be careful with him around Dodge, Liam."

"Believe me, I'm watching my back. Change of subject: Has Arment given you any indications yet about whether I can take up lodging with you once that room is finished?"

"I haven't come straight out and asked him yet. But I will."

At that point Arment came out the door and into the alley where the brothers were talking.

"You know, Mr. Liam, sir, I've been thinking: Joseph told me you were going to be looking for work yourself. Well, there's a wagon shop across town, run by Mr.

Drake Moore, and I know that last week he was talking of needing some help. Do you have any experience with making and repairing wagons?"

"A little, gained during our recent cattle drive, when the sorry chuck wagon broke down three dang times."

"Go talk to him. Tell him I sent you. He may just hire you on."

"I'll do that. Thank you."

"Don't thank me. Thank your brother. If you prove to be half as good a man as he is, I'm doing Drake Moore a favor by sending you his way."

As Liam left, Joseph said to him, privately, "Come by here at the end of the day. I suspect I'll have an answer for you by then about the room. I don't think we'll have any problem at all getting you moved in here, based on Arment's attitude about me and you."

"I'll be by around suppertime."

The wagon shop was easy to find, but Drake himself wasn't. Liam walked through the big double door of the barnlike building that housed the wagon works and called, "Hello? Mr. Moore?"

He received no answer except a series of loud bangs: Someone was hammering on something out back. Liam walked toward the rear door—which, unlike the front entrance, was simply a normal-sized access door—and opened it.

He saw Moore at work on a wagon wheel, hammering a rim into place. His back was turned toward Liam, and it appeared he was unaware Liam was there.

Another man was present, too, watching Moore and also unaware of Liam, and he caught Liam's attention because of the odd fact he wore a masklike covering over half his face. It was somewhat shocking, especially because it was evident that what it covered was more or less a cavity. A part of the man's head apparently was badly malformed or missing.

Liam was shocked and a little more repelled than he could account for. Something tugged at his mind, trying to drag something up from a dim recess somewhere. . . .

He pulled back inside the building and let the door close almost shut. He left it open just enough to allow him to study the masked man without being seen himself.

With Moore occupied and not watching, the masked man, unaware that he was being observed by another, suddenly reached up, lifted back the mask, and scratched at his head in the area the mask had covered.

Liam was jolted. What he saw was clearly the healed-over remnant of a major wartime injury. Part of this man's face had simply been blown away, perhaps by an explosion, maybe by gunfire. There was terribly scarred flesh covering the damaged area, but it was misshapen, ugly. The eye socket was empty and black.

Liam knew how badly war could injure men. He'd come close to suffering such a fate himself when a cannonball exploded near him in a fight outside Nashville. And one time, in the heat of battle, he had himself inflicted—

He gasped loudly, staring at the back of the man's hand as he resettled the mask in place. On that hand was a dark, distinctly shaped birthmark—nothing particularly ugly, but it hammered at Liam's insides even harder than had the glimpse of the man's mangled head and face.

Liam knew that birthmark.

He hurriedly left the barn via the front door. He would not ask for work here today, perhaps not at all. He headed for the nearest saloon and bought himself a bottle.

Suppertime came and went, and Liam did not return to the livery as he'd told Joseph he would. He drank his supper that night and gave no thought to his brother, the room at the livery, or anything at all except a haunted past that had just resurfaced most unexpectedly in the form of a terribly mangled man who could not possibly be still alive, but was.

13

The walls of the new room in the Arment Livery were of unpainted and marvelously scented pine. Through the window, which was turned in the direction away from the often noisy gambling halls and saloons, a cool breeze wafted.

Joseph would have enjoyed a good night's rest in that room, sleeping on the canvas cot Arment had outfitted it with, but despite the fact it was about two in the morning, he wasn't there: He was roaming the streets of Dodge City, looking for his missing brother.

He was deeply worried. Liam was not in his room, and so far not in any of the saloons or similar vice dens. He'd even poked his head into a couple of institutions of ill repute. He was glad he had brought the pistol Liam had given him: Who knew what type of unsavory characters he might run into. No Liam, and no sign of anyone who had seen him.

Joseph, the praying man of the Carrigan family,

prayed more than ever tonight. *Dear Lord, don't let it be Mack Stanley. I pray that sorry, ambushing back-shooter hasn't killed my brother.*

He roamed and searched and prayed, but without apparent result. If Liam was alive and kicking, he was doing his kicking somewhere far from Joseph.

The more time passed, the more worried and depressed Joseph became. A great sense of foreboding hung about him, growing heavier with time. Something was wrong; something had happened.

He was near the freight station when he heard something that caught his attention. A voice, coming from behind the building: It could be Liam's.

Joseph edged a little closer, hopeful but not yet sure that it was Liam's voice he was hearing. If it was, who was he talking to? Some street woman, probably.

Joseph worked his way around an adjacent building, ducked behind a storage shed in the rear, and found an angle from which he could see behind the building. Just as he did so, he heard the suspect voice again—just one of several male voices he could now make out— and realized it was not Liam's.

He could not really see the men, only catch glimpses of movement in the blackness, but he could now hear their whispers. It did not take long to ascertain what they were about to do.

After a couple of minutes the men moved off around the back of the next building and headed toward the railroad freight office. As they rounded the back of the building there was just enough moonlight spilling down to let Joseph make out their silhouettes. Although he could not swear to it, he was almost sure that this was the same group he'd seen on the road outside Dodge.

Where was the law when a man needed it?

Joseph was frustrated. The freight office was at that moment being burglarized, and he couldn't find a marshal or deputy anywhere. It was infuriating, because it meant the burglars would get away with it, and that was intolerable. These were the same men who had stolen from him! They probably had his stolen weapons on them even at that moment.

He finally gave up looking for a lawman and headed toward the freight office himself, driven there not by a plan or even, strictly speaking, a sense of personal duty. In fact, he didn't really consider it his business. A lawman should be handling this, but in the absence of one, what else could he do?

Creeping, sneaking, keeping in the darkest areas, he worked his way around to where he could see through the large side window of the building. They were moving around in there, working in the dark, though on occasion there would be the flare of a match, which was quickly cupped in a hand, then extinguished a moment later.

Joseph heard movement nearby him, outside the building. He shrank down into the shadows beside the elevated porch and reached for his pistol.

One of the grizzled men walked slowly by, shotgun in hand. He was looking around, keeping watch. Joseph should have realized they would post a guard. . . .

He walked within six feet of where Joseph was hiding, holding his breath. Joseph prayed that the pistol, which he'd never fired, was in good working order. If that man turned, saw him, and brought that shotgun up, Joseph would drop him where he stood, without question, warning, or hesitation. He would not let this scoundrel kill him.

The man did not see him. He lingered a few moments, then walked on back the way he had come and around the rear of the building.

Joseph wondered what to do. Part of him wanted to rise, burst in, and demand that the whole bunch of them drop to the floor and spread out. Which was absurd, of course: There were too many of them, all armed, and he would just get himself killed.

Joseph decided to try again to find the law. He'd be glad to lend a hand with the intervention, but the truth was, he didn't really have the authority or training to deal with such a situation.

With the gang's sentinel now around the other side of the building, he was free to move about. He reholstered his pistol, slipped out of his hiding place, and headed for the street—and was greeted by the appearance of a stray dog. Startled, the animal began growling and barking at him.

Joseph froze. *Shut up!* his mind screamed at the barking animal. *Get away from here!*

He heard the sentinel coming back around the building. Joseph was caught. He drew his pistol again as the man turned the corner.

"You there!" the sentinel said, lifting the shotgun. "You, freeze like a statue."

Joseph didn't freeze but swung around and lifted the pistol. "Town marshal," he lied. "You're under arrest."

The man swore; the shotgun went up a few more inches to his shoulder . . .

Joseph fired first. The bullet caught the man squarely in the chest and he went down. The sawed-off shotgun went off as he fell, firing into the sky and sounding like a booming cannon in the enclosed alleyway. The dog quit barking and scrambled under the building like an angry bear diving into a cave.

Inside the freight office, there was a frenzy of activity and a burst of noise as the burglars reacted to the gunshots. Joseph knew that, for just a moment, he held the advantage despite their greater numbers. The burglars were startled and unsure just what had happened. They were inside a building they had no right to be in. If found there by the law, there would be no excuses, nothing ahead but arrest, conviction, and jail time.

"Town marshal!" Joseph yelled. "This building is surrounded by deputies. . . . Come out and surrender your weapons!"

A pane of the big side window shattered, and through the hole a pistol muzzle appeared and spat fire and smoke. The bullet missed Joseph by yards. His own shot was better. He fired back through the glass and heard the pained grunt of the man who took the bullet, and the dropped–feed-sack thud of his body hitting the floor.

There had been six riders. If this was indeed that same group, there were now only four of them left.

Joseph knew better than to stay put, now that they had his location pegged down. He darted around to the rear of the building. He'd hardly rounded the corner before a back door burst open and one of the burglars emerged, trying to take flight while he could, Joseph figured. But nope, not tonight.

"Hold it right there!" Joseph ordered, raising his pistol. The man let out a yell of surprise and froze in place, then was instantly barreled over by another man emerging right on his heels. The first man fell on his face and the second man barely kept his footing. "Hold it!" Joseph yelled again. His heart was racing and his veins flowed with energy; he felt a combination of terror, invigoration, and bewilderment over why he was doing this at all. He could yell "Town marshal!" all he wanted, but he wasn't a town marshal. He was merely a private citizen who'd just broken up a burglary in progress and killed two of the burglars in the process. He'd killed two men! It was inconceivable: He'd killed no one since the war.

The second burglar cursed and fumbled for a pistol in a holster at his hip. "Don't do that!" Joseph yelled.

The man kept on, getting the pistol out . . .

Joseph's shot caught him right in the heart and drove him back into the building, where he collapsed, dead.

Three men dead now.

The first burglar, prone on the little porch landing at the rear door, yelled, "I surrender! Don't shoot!" He thrust his hands in the air while lying on his belly. They bobbed up and down because of his awkward position, making him look like a flapping bird.

"Stay right where you are!" Joseph ordered. "How many more inside?"

"One . . . just one still alive in there."

"There are six in your gang!"

"No . . . just five now. Morgan got mad and left yesterday."

Joseph heard a window smash on the far side of the building, then the sound of someone leaping out and landing, then running.

"Far enough!" a voice called. "You there! Halt where you are or I'll shoot!"

Joseph almost chuckled aloud. At last the law, the real law, was here! The final burglar had just been apprehended.

"Officer!" Joseph shouted at the top of his lungs. "Officer! I've got you one in custody back here! Don't shoot me when you come around! I'm a citizen! I'm on your side, you understand?"

Around the rear of the building came two men, one of them with hands in the air, the other just behind him with a pistol leveled at his back.

"I'm Joseph Carrigan," Joseph said to the lawman with the pistol. "I've got you a prisoner here, and two dead men inside. There's a third dead one around the corner."

"A good evening's work, for a citizen," the lawman said.

"Thank you," Joseph replied. "All I was trying to do was find my brother."

"Even so, you'd best come with me too. We'll have quite a few questions for you."

14

Marshal Charles Bassett had a way of looking at a man that bored right through him like the gaze of God. Try as he would, Joseph couldn't help but feel like a thief and scoundrel himself as Bassett questioned him. The marshal had been off duty that night and soundly sleeping in his bed when he'd been roused by the night deputy and brought down to handle the questioning. This was a major incident that had left three men dead. It was one for the marshal himself to handle, not just a deputy.

Handle it he had. Charles Bassett had left Joseph feeling as if he'd been spitted and put over a slow-roasting fire. The marshal questioned him closely. How had Joseph come to know about the burglary? What had inspired him to involve himself? And what about this claim that one of the burglars was bearing a bone-handled pistol and knife that belonged to him? Did Joseph have ties to this group that he wasn't saying?

Bassett questioned him hard and presented an unreadable face in reaction to each of Joseph's answers. He sent a deputy to rouse Arment from his bed in his house at the edge of town and bring him in to provide whatever information he could about Joseph.

Now it was over . . . perhaps. Bassett was staring at Joseph across a table in his office, his chin propped in his hand. He said nothing, just stared endlessly.

Joseph had the idea that Bassett was waiting for him to say something. He'd wait a long time: Joseph had said all he had to say. He'd told the truth, start to finish, and it was up to Bassett to decide whether to believe him or not.

Finally, Bassett spoke. "Mr. Carrigan, you are either one of the best liars I've ever come across in the ranks of Kansas crime, or you are one of the finest examples of good citizenship I will ever see. I'm inclined to believe the latter. Arment speaks highly of you, and what he says bears much weight with me. He's a smart man who knows people. You can't fool him."

Joseph said nothing.

"Let me ask you something, sir. Have you ever considered a job in law enforcement?"

Joseph blinked, losing the stare-down. This question had surprised him. "I haven't thought about it, sir."

"I want to offer you a job. Nights only. We'll work

with Arment to make sure the schedule doesn't inter-
fere with your livery work."

"What kind of job?"

"Deputy marshal. You'd work from suppertime to
just past midnight. That's when we have most of our
trouble in this town. Most of the job would involve
keeping drunkards from getting overly rowdy. It would
be an easy job for you, given what you've done
tonight."

"What? You'd expect me to shoot drunkards?"

"Of course not. The point is, this thing will be in the
newspaper. You'll have the reputation of a man who
faced down five hard cases and sent three of them to
their graves. We've got tentative identifications on
these gents, by the way. Got it by telegraph out of
Wichita. This gang has done this at other railroad
warehouses. They've killed two night watchmen in the
course of their illustrious careers. You were lucky they
didn't kill you."

"I guess so."

"Or maybe it wasn't luck but skill."

"Or a combination of both. I'm glad for all the prac-
tice and instruction I've had in gunplay in the past. But
I also feel very fortunate indeed. Had a couple of things
gone only slightly different, I might be dead."

"I don't dispute you there. Anytime you go up
against men like these, you run the risk of shortening
your life. Goes with the job. Which brings me back to

the question of the morning: Would you be interested in being a part-time deputy?"

Joseph tried to picture himself out at night on the streets of Dodge City, gun strapped to his waist, badge on his vest, his reputation preceding him everywhere he went. Both a good thing and a bad one, that would be. From some it might provoke violence, prideful efforts to overcome the lawman who'd gunned down three bad men in the dark of night. But from most it would surely generate awe and respect.

He was indeed interested in the job. But he needed time to think it over and to talk it through with Liam.

"Give me a day to decide," he said.

"Fair enough."

"I can go now?"

"Yes . . . but one more question: What's the first name of that brother you were out looking for?"

"Liam."

"Ah, yes. I figured as much. Come with me back to the cells."

"You're locking me up?"

"Of course not. But there's somebody back here I'd like to turn over to your custody. Remember what I said about rounding up rowdy drunks?"

"Downright embarrassing," Joseph said in a disgusted tone as he walked beside the still-staggering

Liam, whom he'd just collected from Bassett's cell. "Here I am, getting offered a job as a lawman, and my own brother is at that very moment locked up for roaming drunk on the streets."

"I didn't hurt anybody. It's my business what I do."

"I guess it is. It's still embarrassing, under the circumstances."

They walked along in silence a few minutes more. "Where are we going? This ain't the way to my place."

"Your place is going to be at my place from now on. I talked to Arment today: He's got no objection to you staying at the livery with me at night. There's only one cot at the moment, though. You'll have to throw a blanket on the floor."

"Nice of him. I'll start paying him as soon as I get work." Liam was getting over his drunkenness, but his voice remained slurred.

"Did you go to the wagon shop today?"

Liam paused. "I did."

"No luck, huh?"

"No."

"Liam, you didn't go out and get drunk just because you got turned down for a job?"

"No." Liam waited for Joseph to ask the inevitable next question, but it didn't come.

"You aren't going to ask me why I did get drunk?"

"No. I've been mulling it over, Liam. I'm going to

leave you in peace. I guess I've tried a little too hard to be my brother's keeper."

"That you have."

"You're all the family I've got, Liam."

"Except maybe Uncle Patrick."

"Maybe." Joseph stopped cold in the middle of the street, staring straight ahead.

"What's wrong?" Liam asked.

Joseph turned, staggered to the left, leaned over, and heaved his stomach empty onto the street.

"You sick?" Liam asked.

"God, Liam, I killed men tonight. God!"

Liam nodded. "I know. I could hear you and the marshal talking."

"I was just out looking for you, Liam. That's all. I was afraid that Mack Stanley had killed you."

"It'd take more than him to kill me."

"Look at me, Liam. I'm shaking."

"I remember, Joseph. I recollect what it's like. It was that way for me during the war. You do what you have to do, and it's only later that it all comes down on top of you and you feel like you're getting crushed really slow. I remember that. And I remember the trembling."

Joseph lifted his hand and watched it shake. His mouth was full of the acrid taste of vomit.

"I'm glad you came through it all safe and sound tonight, Joseph. You could have gotten killed, easy. Why did you do it?"

"I don't know, Liam. I didn't plan it. I was just trying to figure out what to do, and all at once they knew I was there, and it all just started up."

"You fought a good fight, soldier." Liam hiccuped and staggered a little on his feet.

Joseph shook his head and made no reply. He was looking off into the darkness, thinking thoughts he would not speak aloud.

"You going to take the lawman job?" Liam asked.

"I don't know."

"You ought to do it. Once the story spreads about tonight, you'll be a town hero. Not a man would dare to cross you."

"I don't want to talk about this right now. I just want some sleep."

"You'd make a good lawman."

"You think so?"

"I've always thought you would. Hell, lawmen are all devoted to rules and such, right? That's you all over."

"Come on. Let's get on to the livery and maybe get at least an hour or two of sleep tonight."

They walked on, reaching the livery. Joseph dug in his pocket for his key.

"By the way, I didn't get turned down for that job at the wagon shop," Liam said. "I never asked."

"Why not?"

"I saw somebody there that I had . . . somebody I met back during the war."

"Got to talking, huh?"

"No. Not with this man."

"Who was it?"

Liam paused. "I'll tell you about it in the morning. It's too big a thing to talk about when you're drunk and tired."

"You going back to the wagon shop again?"

"Tomorrow."

"You got me wondering about this man you saw."

"I'll tell you about it in the morning."

They went inside and locked the door behind them.

15

The next morning came much too early. Joseph awakened to the sound of Arment opening the outer doors and leaped out of his bunk to dress quickly. Liam had slept on a blanket tossed across a stack of empty feed sacks. He woke up with his head throbbing and groaned as he rose.

"No need for you to get up that I can see," Joseph said. "Go ahead and sleep it off."

"No," Liam said. "You rise, I rise. I've done enough lying around lately."

"Suit yourself."

"Joseph, you going to do it?"

"What?"

"Take the deputy job."

Joseph paused, then nodded. "I think I will. With you here at night, the livery will still be guarded. I can make some more money, get us back on our feet a little quicker."

"Will Arment go along?"

"I think so."

"You'll do a good job of it."

"Thank you."

Arment was gracious as Liam thanked him for allowing him to lodge with his brother. "I'll be scouting around for work today," he said, struggling to look alert and pain-free despite his night of drinking. "I'll pay you as quick as I can."

"No need for it. It ain't costing me a thing for you to sleep here. I wish I could hire you myself, to tell the truth. But one man is all I can afford to pay."

"You've got more than a man in my brother here," Liam said, slapping Joseph's shoulder lightly. "This man is a hero. He had quite an adventure last night. Well, I'm going out back to wash up in the trough, then I'm off to meet Drake Moore."

He did just that and was gone for an hour before Joseph realized he'd never asked Liam to tell him the story he'd been too tired to tell the night before.

Drake Moore eyed Liam Carrigan from head to toe. Stout-looking. Strong hands, callused. The weathered face of a man who knew work. Nothing to make Drake say an immediate no to his request for a job.

"So what experience do you have with wagons?" Drake asked.

"Mostly work on the ones we had when I was growing up, and on the chuck wagon on a cattle drive I was on along the Chisholm Trail. It broke down a lot, and it always seemed to fall to me to fix it."

"If it broke down a lot, you must not have been fixing it too well, huh?"

He had him there. Liam couldn't think of an answer right away. "Well," he said, "we didn't have the good tools you have here. And it was a very old wagon."

"Well, that would make a difference. I've found the main thing ain't always experience but the willingness to learn."

"I'm willing. I'll learn whatever I need. I just need the work, Mr. Moore."

"Call me Drake."

"All right."

"If I hired you, when could you commence?"

"Right away, I reckon."

Moore rubbed his chin whiskers. "I told you what I pay. . . . Enough for you?"

"It's enough." At present, Liam would settle for almost any amount.

"Consider yourself hired, then. We'll try it a couple of weeks and see how you come along. If you can learn the work, and if it still suits you, and if you're still suiting me, well, we'll just keep going."

Four hours later, Liam was a weary man. But he would not let it show. He worked hard, determined to make Drake glad he'd hired him.

In mid-afternoon they took a few minutes off to enjoy coffee that Moore had brewed. Sipping it, Liam threw in a comment as casually as possible. "You know, I came by here yesterday."

"I never seen you."

"No. I was going to ask you about work, but I thought you'd filled the job already."

"Why'd you think that?"

"Saw a man here. It looked like he was working with you. I figured he'd been hired."

"Well, no, he wasn't. I had three or four different gents come by yesterday, but all of them were paying customers. Well, all but one."

"What do you mean?"

"There's one gent, really a pitiful fellow, who is poor as the church mouse's cousin. I do work for him for free. We both pretend he'll pay me later on, but we know he won't."

"It's kind of you to help him."

"This gent needs all the help he can get. He's had a hard row to hoe in life. The war took part of his face away. He wears a kind of mask now."

Liam lifted the cup to his lips for another swallow of coffee. He felt very nervous. "That's the man I saw," he said. "I wondered why he wore that thing."

"I've never seen what's under it," Moore said. "Them who have say it's an ugly sight. Poor fellow pretty much stays away from folks. He lives with his family out in a sod house somewhere, raising wheat and chickens and a few head of cattle. He don't make much of a living. There's some church folks who make sure the family is fed when times get really hard."

"What's the name of this fellow?"

"Scott. Mordecai Scott. They say he was a Union soldier in the war. They say he lost his face to a shotgun blast in Tennessee. Hey, why are your hands trembling so?"

"The work, you know," Liam said. "You know how when you work with your hands sometimes. straining your muscles and all, they'll shake. Mordecai Scott, huh?"

"That's right. Why did you think he was working for me?"

"I don't know. Hey, I think I'll have a little more coffee. How big a family does this Scott fellow have?"

"A wife and two sons. I think that's the whole bunch of them. Why are you so interested?"

Liam paused. "He reminds me of someone I knew during the war."

"Well, a man should be kind to them who have been dealt a bad hand by life. That's the Bible way, it seems to me. That's why I do free work for him. I just wish other folks would be as kind."

"He's treated bad?"

"It's awful to see. Children throw rocks at him. Right there in the open, right on the street in front of God and everybody! They pick fights with his boys. I've seen that wife of his weep like a baby. It'll break your heart, I tell you."

Liam stared into his coffee cup without speaking.

"People can be mighty mean," Moore said.

"Yeah," Liam said. "Yeah, they can."

The story of Joseph's single-handed victory over the gang of burglars filled much of the newspaper that afternoon and was read and reread all across Ford County. Arment read it aloud to Joseph, pausing to give commentary about every third line, most of it to the effect that Joseph's life would not be the same again. He was a hero now.

Over at the wagon works, Moore also read the newspaper account aloud for Liam. He wasn't a good reader, and it was all Liam could do to keep from snatching the paper away from his boss to read it for himself. He suffered through Moore's stammering schoolboy presentation and wondered how Joseph was reacting to all of this sudden public praise.

When at last Moore finished the account and put the paper down, he said, "Ain't it something that this brother of yours has gone from town stranger to town hero! Why, right now he's probably more feared and respected than Charlie Bassett himself, or Bat Masterson! How you reckon he feels about that, huh?"

"I daresay he feels like it was all his destiny. Everything that happens to him, he believes it's his destiny or his fate playing itself out. If he found a penny in an outhouse, he'd figure that his urge to piss was really his destiny leading him to be where he needed to be to find that coin. He's thought like that since he was a little boy. Nothing just happens to Joseph. He draws grand conclusions about everything and sees patterns everywhere he looks."

"Well, maybe he's right. Not about the penny in the outhouse and such, but about the bigger things, anyway."

"Well, if this is destiny, then all I have to say is that destiny ain't always kind. It gives fame and heroism to some. Others just get reminded of things they wish had never happened."

"What the devil are you talking about?"

"Nothing. Hey, ain't there work to do around here? Or are we just going to sit around reading the newspaper all day?"

"I'm the boss around here. If I say we read the paper, we read the paper." He rose and began preparing to put the second coat of paint on a surrey that a customer was due to pick up later in the day.

"Moody, I reckon!" Moore muttered beneath his breath. "Moody as a dang woman, I swear."

Liam was walking back to the livery when he saw her. She stood on a boardwalk, looking very small and pale in the evening light. She stared at him as he crossed the street, and he stopped and looked back at her for several moments.

She approached, and the nearer she got, the more scared she looked. Still she kept on until she stood before him, about four feet away.

"I'm mighty sorry," she said. "I shouldn't have done it. But I can't say no to him. If you say no to him, he hurts you."

"Is that right . . . Lilly? It is Lilly, ain't it? As I recall it, he indicated you did it for money."

She hung her head. "I have to have money just like anybody does."

"He would have killed me, you know."

"I didn't know he'd do that, sir. I swear it. I didn't know."

He was inclined to believe her. But did it matter much? She surely had known that Mack Stanley had intended to hurt him, at the very least.

"You want me to say I forgive you for it? All right. I do. But if you want to make up for it . . ."

She took a step forward. "Whatever you want. No charge."

"Lord, girl, that's not what I'm talking about. I was going to ask you for information. Tell me where Mack is now."

"I don't know. God's truth, I don't. I ain't seen him since it happened."

"If you do see him, you can help me out by letting me know. If he gets the chance to back-shoot me, he'll do it. He already tried it once."

"You mean, since the alley?"

"No. Before that. He's tried to kill me twice. "

"Why does he hate you?"

"He worked for me and my brother, during a cattle drive. We had a dispute."

"I hate him. I'm afraid of him."

"Did you know him before he hired you to lure me?"

"Yes. I've known him for two years. He'd come and go, following the cattle trails. When he's here he finds me. He told me once he loved me. I know now he lied to me."

"He's a bad man. Stay away from him."

"He won't stay away from me."

Liam considered telling her where he lived and to come to him there at the livery should Stanley return. But he couldn't trust her. She might lead Stanley to him by accident or design.

"If he comes back, you tell my brother. His name is Joseph Carrigan, and he's going to be a town deputy marshal. You get to the marshal's office and tell him."

She looked frightened and shook her head sharply. "I don't talk to the law," she said. "I don't never do that. But if he comes back, I'll try to warn you."

She turned and hurried away, shoulders lowered as if she were trying to sink into herself. Liam watched her go and wondered how so young and pretty a girl could find herself in such a desperate situation that she had turned to a life of whoring. Had she no family—no one to provide for her? Where had she come from?

Maybe he'd have the chance to ask her, sometime later. He watched her until she had turned a corner and was out of sight.

When Liam arrived at the livery, Arment was still there, having stayed late to work on a saddle. Joseph was gone.

"He's taken that deputy job," Arment explained, so proud of his new and highly favored employee that his chest was swelling. "It's a fine thing—makes me proud of him. He'll be working evenings from when he finishes here, on to about midnight most nights of the week. Here . . . take this key. You'll be needing it to get in and out, especially since Joseph won't be around as much. Did the wagon works job work out for you?"

"Yes. Moore seems to be a good man."

"An excellent one. Well, I'm through for the evening. Maybe I'll see you in the morning."

"I doubt it. I'll be going in early to work."

When Arment was gone, Liam pondered that he'd not see Joseph nearly as much. He'd be out making his deputy rounds in the evenings when Liam got back from work.

Liam did not go out to the saloons that night. He

was tired from the day's labor, and Lilly weighed heavily on his mind. Despite her betrayal of him to Mack Stanley, he felt far more pity than anger toward her. When he'd told her he forgave her, he'd meant it.

He was asleep when Joseph came in after midnight, moving quietly. Liam did not awaken.

16

Two nights later the moon was hidden by clouds, making the streets darker and the saloons and dance halls brighter. Joseph Carrigan, wearing his badge, roamed from one den of vice to another, playing the lawman for Charles Bassett. At each stop he was greeted by men who either slapped his back in admiration or looked on in awed respect. Every female stared at him as though he were a god. Amazing, what gunning down a few criminals could do for a man's reputation.

But it all seemed unreal, dreamlike. It felt more as though he were observing it all from outside himself than actually experiencing it.

As a lawman, he had the privilege of going armed in a town that denied that right to others—and for good reason, given the amount of liquor that flowed in Dodge City. But the pistol he wore was not the bone-handled Colt that had been stolen by, then recovered from, the burglar gang. He wore the one that Liam had seized from Mack Stanley. It was a less flashy weapon. The gleaming bone-handled Colt had always tended to draw notice and admiration; men wanted to look at it and heft it in their hands and talk about what a fine piece of work it was. Right now Joseph didn't want that. He was already perceived, against his wishes, as a heroic gunman. He didn't need to carry a pistol that only heightened that image.

All the veneration would fade with time, he supposed. He looked forward to that, but with apprehension mixed in. As the notoriety faded, so would fear of him. And life might grow more dangerous.

It didn't matter. He'd already decided that his time as a lawman would be brief. He was doing this only for the moment, and for the money—and for Arment, who was extraordinarily proud of having a hero working for him and living in a room right there in his own livery stable. The way Arment had been going on for the past couple of days, Joseph wouldn't be surprised if the livery stableman put up a brass plaque on the door of the sleeping quarters after Joseph moved on from Dodge: JOSEPH CARRIGAN, THE HERO OF DODGE CITY AND BANE TO THIEVES, SLEPT HERE.

Sleep there he did, hard and deeply, every night. After a day of shoveling out stalls and brushing down horses and hefting heavy saddles on and off, followed by a few hours of trudging up and down the streets of

Dodge's seamier districts, Joseph slept like a dead man. Liam did the same: For the past two nights he'd been snoring his head off when Joseph got in from making the rounds. Their interactions had been limited to early mornings, when both were getting ready for their day's work. Liam would clean up, run down to a café, and bring back eggs and biscuits for their breakfast; they would talk briefly and superficially while they ate, and Liam would be off to the wagon works.

At length, Joseph's allotted hours as a deputy marshal ticked off for one more day, and he headed gladly for his bed in the livery. Liam was there, asleep as usual.

That night, however, Joseph did not sleep deeply and dreamlessly as usual. He had a vague stomachache that kept him from fully relaxing. He had dreams, and not good ones. He was back in the war again, in his blue Union uniform, dodging cannonballs and bullets. Then suddenly he was outside the freight house again, shooting at burglars, but this time with pistols that fired haphazardly and couldn't be aimed. He dreamed he was looking down the wrong end of a sawed-off shotgun that was about to blow his head off. He woke up in a sweat.

Joseph sat up in bed. By the moonlight streaming through his window he read his pocket watch. Three in the morning, on the dot.

He almost dropped the watch when Liam bolted up suddenly in his blankets, yelling and clawing at his face.

"No!" Liam yelled. "No, no!"

"Liam!" Joseph exclaimed sharply. "Wake up—you're dreaming!"

Liam jerked his head around and stared at Joseph. His face transformed as he slowly awakened. "Good Lord . . . what a nightmare!"

"Must have been. I thought you'd tear your face off."

Liam, breathing heavily, shook his head. "Don't say that."

"Are you all right?"

"Yeah. Yeah. Just a dream."

"I haven't had a chance to talk to you much since I started the deputy work."

"No."

"The wagon job going well?"

"I'm learning a lot. I seem to suit Drake." He shook his head like a wet dog. "God help me, what a dream!"

"What was it?"

"I dreamed a man shot my face off with a shotgun. During the war."

"I dream about the war too."

"I know. I've heard you talk and yell in your sleep sometimes."

"Really?" Joseph looked away. "Kind of embarrassing."

"Don't be embarrassed. I just sat up in bed clawing my face like a fool. I hope I didn't scratch it up. You care if I have a smoke to settle my nerves?"

"Go ahead."

When the small cigar was glowing red in the darkness, Liam spoke again.

"There's been something I've been wanting to tell you for two, three days now, and there hasn't been a chance."

"That thing you were going to tell me the night of the big shooting?"

"That's right." Liam drew on the cigar. "I got drunk that night because I'd seen Mordecai Scott."

"Who?"

"Mordecai Scott. The man with the ruined face."

"Oh, yes. Poor wretch. But why would you get drunk just over seeing him? The war left a lot of men mangled up."

"Yes . . . but he's the only one who is mangled up because of me."

"What?"

"I'm the one who did it, Joseph. I'm the one who shot that poor man's face all to hell with a shotgun. I never knew he lived through it until I saw him outside the wagon shop the first time I went to ask for work. It hit me like a falling stone when I realized who he was."

Joseph was trying to make sense of it. "Wait, Liam.

There's no way you could know it's the same man—not if his face is mangled up."

"I didn't know him by his face. He has a mark on his hand. I saw that mark clearly when I was fighting him hand to hand before I shot him. And I saw it when he raised his hand to wipe sweat off his face—what's left of it. I saw the face, too, because he lifted the hood. He didn't know I was there. God, it's awful what I did to him."

"That accounts for the dream you just had."

"Yes. The man shooting me in the dream was Mordecai Scott."

"Tell me how it all happened."

"Might take a few minutes. Can you spare the sleep?"

"I can spare it. But if you're right about this, it's amazing. What are the odds that you two would cross paths again?"

"I figure they're slimmer than the odds he could have even lived through such a horrible wound. But he did live . . . and now here we are in the same county. So now I'm starting to think like you. I'm thinking that maybe it ain't a matter of odds but of destiny, or pre-destination, or whatever you call it. Maybe I was sup-posed to run across him again."

"For what reason, though?"

"So I can help him. Make up for what I did to him."

"You must not feel guilty for what you did, Liam. It was war. Kill or be killed."

"I know. But I didn't kill him; that's the point: I just mangled him awful. Lord, when I think what that man must have suffered all these years, going through life so chewed up that he can't even show his face . . ."

"It was a shotgun, you say? Since when did you Rebs fight the war with shotguns?"

"It was an old smoothbore, a farmhouse weapon. I didn't know what it was loaded with, but it turned out to be shot. This all happened in a skirmish, not a battle. Five or six of us on either side. We were shooting at each other, fighting hand to hand in a couple of cases. I saw one of the Yanks run into this farmhouse. It was empty: The family had fled. I followed the Yank inside. We fired off our weapons at each other, both of us missing. It was hand-to-hand after that. He came out with a knife and slashed at me. He cut me right across the belly—not deep, but it bled. You've seen the scar yourself."

"You never would tell me how you got it. I figured it was a woman or a jealous husband."

"Well, now you know. Anyway, I got the knife away from him, but he knocked it back out of my hand and it landed over behind some furniture where we couldn't get to it. Scott and me struggled and fought and did our best to kill each other bare-handed, but we couldn't do it. All this time I'm thinking how strange it is to be fighting with a man I don't know, for reasons I don't really understand, when in another situation we might be taking a drink together in a saloon. Funny how you can think like that while you're fighting for your life. Somewhere along the way, I bump up against a wardrobe and the doors open up and this shotgun falls out. I got hold of it, yanked it up . . . I don't remember firing it, but I did. It was as loud as a cannon, and this poor fellow fell back clawing at his face . . . but the face wasn't really there anymore." Liam paused and shuddered. "There were parts of it hanging off of him, Joseph. Hanging off like pieces of loose meat. And his hand just groping at it, and me staring at the birthmark until blood covered it up so you couldn't see it no more. . . . God. God."

Joseph drew in a long breath and blew it out slowly through rounded lips.

"He grabbed at that face, rolling around, not screaming or anything . . . just groaning. Terrible groans. Then he lay still. No moving, no breathing that I could see. I was sure he was dead. I didn't check him close: There seemed no need for it, and I had to get back outside to help against the others. Besides, he was my enemy. I wasn't supposed to care whether he was dead. You know how it is in wartime."

"I know."

"Anyway, the skirmish broke up after that. None of my group was killed. One man wounded slightly. The

Yanks all got away, except for the one I shot . . . except for Scott."

"It wasn't your fault, Liam. It was war."

"I know. But it was still me who did it. And now, out of the blue, here I am again, and here he is."

"But why do you think you'd be brought together with him after all these years? What would be the purpose in it? You can't undo what was done."

"I've been thinking on that lately. It seems to me that sometimes things a man did in the past are like unsettled accounts. They come back up due and payable, and you have to deal with them. I think maybe I'm supposed to do something to help Scott and his family. And I swear I'm going to do it. It's why the good Lord brought me to Dodge City. I believe it to be a fact."

Joseph was surprised to hear his generally faithless brother talking in such a way. "But what can you do for them?"

"I don't know. I'll think of something."

"Do you know where they live?"

"Not exactly. I can find them, though."

"Will you tell Scott who you are?"

"I don't know. I'll have to just see how that all falls out."

"What if he knows you?"

"He might, but probably not. If not for him having that mark on his hand and being wounded in such a specific way, I'd never know him. He'd be just another stranger, one more in the blur of all the other strangers you see in war. You know, I've sat at bars many a time sipping whiskey and sharing laughs with strangers I just met, and wondering if at some time along the way the two of us shot at each other across a battlefield. It's a strange and wicked thing, war."

"Maybe you should think awhile before you go find Scott. You don't know what he'll think about it. You don't know what he'll do."

"I have to do it, Joseph. I've wrestled with it since I saw him."

"Then you should do it. Want me to help you?"

"Thank you, Joseph. But I think this is one I'm supposed to do alone."

"Liam, Arment keeps a little bottle of brandy in his desk inside. He's not the kind who minds sharing. If you'd like a little of it, he'd not care at all."

Liam nodded and crushed out his cigar on the floor. "I believe I will. It might be just the thing to help me sleep. I've talked so much that I've wore off my tiredness. You ought to take some too. For sleeping medicine."

Joseph, the nondrinker, thought about it. "Sleeping medicine. Sounds good to me. Come on in. I'll find us a couple of medicine cups."

Minutes later they stood by the window with brandy in coffee cups, moonlight streaming in around them.

"Here's to Liam Carrigan, and to his mission," Joseph said.

"And here's to Joseph Carrigan, heroic lawman of Dodge City," Liam replied.

"May both succeed."

"Indeed."

They clinked the cups together and drank.

17

Another day of work, this one harder than most. Another evening of walking Front Street and Dodge's other avenues and alleyways of vice, wearing a badge and looking for trouble he hoped he wouldn't find. Joseph was a reluctant lawman on the prowl through town, protected only by his own wits and the lingering respect he'd earned as a marksman.

But Joseph had a bad feeling about tonight. Couldn't account for it, but couldn't shake it.

He was an hour away from his quitting time when the trouble he had anticipated finally found him.

It was quite a disappointment. The night had been so unusually quiet until then that Joseph was persuaded that his premonition of trouble hadn't been a premonition at all, just worry brought on by too much work and the stress of that blasted gunfight he couldn't get past.

When he walked into the Long Branch Saloon, his hopes were dashed. The place was quiet, but only because the patrons were too busy watching a performance to make much noise. The performance consisted of a huge, bald, very drunk man with the shoulders of a miner or a railroad track layer busily pounding the head of a much smaller man against the side of the bar. *Whump, whump, whump.* Not a soul was lifting a finger to intervene.

The little man was still conscious, but it didn't appear he would be much longer. He was unarmed. The man injuring him was not. A Remington pistol was holstered at his side.

For a moment Joseph simply froze in surprise at this odd and disturbing scene, then stepped forward. "You there, stop that!" he ordered.

The bald man ignored him. Joseph advanced, grabbed the man's shoulder, and pulled him around to face him. "I told you to stop that!"

Eyes bleary and red looked back at Joseph, and breath so alcoholic it was probably flammable buffeted his face. "I can't stop. I got to kill this man."

"No. Let him go."

The bald man frowned, then let go of the man, who collapsed to the floor, whimpering. He lay there a moment, then rose, gripping his head, and staggered in a rush to the door and out into the night.

"But I got to kill him," the bald man slurred out

again, actually sounding a little plaintive. "He stole horses from me."

"You'll not kill anyone in Dodge."

The man drew his pistol. "I got to go after him."

Joseph backed up a step and drew his own weapon. "Drop that pistol, friend, right now. You cannot carry a pistol here. You're in violation of the town ordinance."

The man cocked his head and looked at Joseph as if he were some bizarre, unexplainable oddity, like a talking dog. "I got to kill him," he repeated.

"Listen to me: Drop the pistol!" Joseph leveled his own pistol at the man.

Drunkenly, the fellow simply stood there with his idiotic frown, neither dropping nor raising the pistol. He looked in puzzlement at Joseph, then at the door through which his victim had fled, then back at Joseph again.

"Does anybody here know this man?" Joseph asked the crowd around him, which had backed away a considerable distance now that pistols had come out.

No one answered. Joseph bellowed out his question again. This time someone said, "He's a stranger, as far as I know."

"Watch out for him, Mr. Carrigan," another voice said. "He's so drunk he don't even know where he is."

"What's your name, mister?" Joseph asked the man he was looking at down the length of his pistol.

"I got to go," the man said, stepping forward as if to bypass Joseph. "I got to go kill him."

"Drop the pistol!" Joseph demanded again, this time nearly in a shout. "Drop it or I'll be forced to shoot you!"

The man paused and looked at him dumbly, and Joseph wondered if he was dealing with a mere drunkard or a man who was mentally deficient as well. Either way or both, he was very dangerous.

Abruptly something changed in the man's expression. The dull quality vanished in a moment and was replaced by a viscious snarl of anger. "Don't you point no damn pistol at me!" he growled.

The drunkard's Remington came up. He tried to aim it at Joseph, but it wavered and moved as if the very floor beneath his feet was pitching like a ship in a storm.

"You better shoot him, Mr. Carrigan," someone in the crowd advised.

"Drop it!" Joseph barked.

The pistol continued to wave, then went off. The shot was high and wild and passed out through the wall into the night sky. It sent everyone in the place, except the shooter and Joseph, scrambling back and down and into any safe spot that could be found.

The drunkard laughed, apparently surprised by his own shot, then took hold of the pistol with both hands and managed to gain better control of it. He aimed it at Joseph.

"Shoot him!" someone yelled.

Joseph raised his Colt, took aim . . . but something made him freeze. He didn't fire.

The bald man laughed again and squinted down the barrel of his gun.

From behind him the barkeep appeared as if from nowhere, a short bat of maplewood in his hand. He struck the man on the back of the head and drove him to his knees. The hand holding the pistol dropped, and the gun fired into the floor. The barkeep kicked it, driving it out of the man's hand. It scooted off across the floor, spinning.

"Get up from there," the barkeep ordered. "Let this deputy take you to the jail, where you belong."

The drunkard's hand came up, bearing a knife. No one had seen him pull it from beneath his vest.

"He's got a knife!" somebody yelled. "Shoot him, Carrigan!"

The man stuck the knife deeply into the barkeep's belly.

Joseph fired just in time, the bullet piercing the hand of the drunkard and sending the knife spinning off, surrounded by a spray of red. The drunkard did not scream or even grunt. He simply looked at the hole in his hand and watched the blood gush out of it.

"I'll be!" he said, standing and waving the bleeding hand around for all to see. "Kind of reminds you of the hand of Jesus, don't it!" Then he fainted from a combination of mounting shock and far too much alcohol.

Joseph stared at him, still holding the pistol.

"He stabbed me," the barkeep said. "Why didn't you shoot him?"

"I did."

"Not quick enough." The barkeep staggered to the nearest chair and flopped down.

"Somebody, get a doctor!" a woman said, and two men rushed out of the saloon to do it.

"You balked, Carrigan," a man said. "If you'd fired faster, he'd not have stabbed him."

"I didn't balk."

"The hell!"

The barkeep laid his head over on the table and looked very weak. He was bleeding a lot, as was the passed-out drunk on the floor.

"I better go make sure they really went after a doctor," Joseph said. He holstered the pistol and left quickly.

Caleb Arment lived on the edge of Dodge City and walked to the livery each morning that the weather was good. On rainy days he would come in on a wagon he'd outfitted with a somewhat frilly parasol-type cover, a rig that had gotten a few laughs until folks got used to seeing it.

That morning was a wagon morning. It wasn't raining yet, but clouds were thickening, the breeze was rising, cool and damp, and Arment had no confidence that he could make it all the way to the livery before the sky opened up. So he rode through town, aboard his wagon, sipping coffee he'd brought from home in a big crockery cup. He'd make a new potful at the livery as soon as he got there, unless Joseph had done it already. Arment loved Joseph's Arbuckles' coffee.

Joseph hadn't made the coffee and in fact was just opening the livery doors when Arment arrived. Arment glanced at his pocket watch: Joseph was opening ten minutes late. He hesitated, then decided not to ask why. Joseph had probably just overslept. It wasn't typical, so he'd let it pass this time.

Joseph looked at his employer and gave a feeble smile of greeting. Arment noticed that he looked tired and drawn.

"Morning, Joseph. How are you?"

"Needing coffee. Sorry I slept too late. I'm behind time getting us open."

Arment climbed down from the wagon. Joseph was already beginning to unhitch the horse. "Ah, well, no harm done this once," Arment said. "Are you feeling poorly?"

"I'm well."

"Slept soundly?"

"Not too well last night."

"Ah, yeah." Arment wanted to ask why, but something his wife continually told him about him being too nosy came to mind and shut him up. "Liam's gone to his work, I guess."

"He was gone before I got up."

Arment went inside and put coffee on to boil. Joseph finished putting up the horse and set to work repairing the wall of a damaged stall.

Arment picked up an old copy of the newspaper and pretended to read it while actually observing Joseph. The young man was not himself today, to be sure. He worked steadily but without spirit, and had little to say. Several attempts to spark up conversation fizzled out like fire in a thunderstorm.

At last, Arment's restraint gave way. "Dang, Joseph, you're either sickly or you've lost a loved one. What the devil's wrong with you?"

Joseph looked at his boss, his eyes flashing in anger at Arment's intrusiveness. But it was a passing moment. He seemed to wilt a little more. "Nothing's wrong," he said. "Just tired today from not sleeping well."

"Ain't nothing wrong with Liam, is there?"

"No. Not that I know of."

"Well . . . sorry to be so inquisitional." Arment went back to his paper.

Despite his mood, Joseph had to smile. Arment had an unwitting way of butchering the language that was often entertaining.

Arment's own mood declined because of Joseph's brooding. He went to work on the books, found that task irritating, and put it aside to return to repairing a saddle he'd been working on as a long-term project for weeks now. He'd sell it for a nice profit when it was done.

At about ten in the morning Charles Bassett came calling. "Going to rain, boys," he said as he walked in.

Arment was surprised to see the town marshal, who seldom came around unless there was a problem of some sort. Bassett had little to say to Arment. He'd come to talk to Joseph.

Joseph glanced at Arment and led Bassett outside. By all indications the rain that was threatening would be there in minutes, but it hadn't come yet. Joseph obviously wanted his conversation with Bassett to be carried on privately.

Arment fought a quick battle with conscience; conscience lost, and the liveryman headed for the loft and the open window up there through which he could hear what the pair outside were talking about.

"Who told you about it?" Joseph was saying by the time Arment got into listening position.

"Three or four folks around town. It's kind of the talk this morning. They're saying that you lost your nerve. You hesitated when there was no time for it, and we nearly lost us a barman."

"Is he all right?"

"He'll live, but the doc says the knife did some bad damage. It could have killed him."

"He really shouldn't have gotten involved. I had the situation in hand."

"I was told the barkeep went after him with a club because you weren't moving fast enough. Then, when it was time to shoot, you waited until it was almost too late."

"My pistol jammed."

"Did it? I was told you never even tried to fire until the barkeep was already stabbed."

"I did try. It didn't fire the first time. I tried again and it did. So what's this interrogation about, Marshal? Nobody's dead. I fired a shot and saved a man's life. I don't know what the hell has you so unhappy."

"Don't waste your time getting angry with me, Joseph. I have to talk to you about this. It's my duty to this town, and to them who work for me, to make sure that everyone is up to their snuff. This work is dangerous, and I don't relish having a deputy shot down because he balks when it's time to pull a trigger."

Thunder rumbled off in the west. The sky was very gray.

"I told you: My pistol jammed."

"Have you worked on it?"

"No."

"Better let me see it, then. I've got some skill in putting guns back in fix."

"What I meant was, I haven't worked on it yet. But I left it at the gunsmith's shop this morning for him to look at."

In the loft, Arment lifted a brow. Joseph had done no

158

such thing. He'd been at the livery since he got up.

"Will the pistol be ready for you by this evening?"

"Yes. And if it ain't, I've got a second I can use."

"I'll talk to you straight, Joseph: Your reputation has taken a hard lick. People are talking. You're not seen as the fearless pistoleer they've thought you to be up until now."

Another peal of thunder pierced the air. Bassett glanced at the sky, then locked his steel gaze onto Joseph again.

"So you took that jamming pistol to the gunsmith shop, did you?"

"Yes. This morning."

"Son, the gunsmith's closed today. Been closed all week. Henry is out of town."

Joseph opened his mouth but found nothing to say. Bassett had caught him cold.

"Joseph, let's not lie to each other. In this line of work a man can't afford lies, either telling them or hearing them. And a man can't let his pride keep him from admitting when he's blundered. You were lucky last night that you or somebody else didn't get killed. You should have shot that man well before things went as far as they did. I think you know that."

"I didn't want to kill a man who didn't know what he was doing. He was drunk out of his mind."

"Which made him a danger to you and the public. By the way, he don't remember a thing that happened last night. He's lying over in the jail with his hand in a bandage and a headache as big as St. Louis. Now I've got to ask you something, Joseph: Are you up to do this job? Can you go back out on the street tonight and do what has to be done, even if it means killing a man?"

Joseph thought about it. He'd been ready to leave the deputy work behind at any point. Only his employment promises to Bassett, his pride, and his need for all the money he could earn had kept him at the task.

He could walk away right now. Bassett was inviting him to do so, if he wanted to.

But he couldn't walk away. All the reasons that had kept him on the job until now still held, with a new one added: To leave the job now would mark his reputation in this town forever. He'd be labeled as yellow, a man who threw away his badge the first time he encountered a problem. This latter incident would grow to overshadow what had happened before. The public hero would become the public joke.

He had to keep going.

"I'm ready to do the job, Marshal," he said.

He'd wondered how Bassett would react to that. Maybe he'd wanted him to quit. But Bassett grinned.

"Good. Good." Bassett paused, and his tone changed. "Happened to me once, you know. I just froze up. Fortunately, the man on the other side of the equation was so sorry a shot that he missed me by a yard. Another man with me brought him down with a single shot from a Henry repeater. It ain't a story I often tell."

Arment was back at work on the saddle by the time Joseph got back inside. Not a word was said about what had just transpired. Joseph wondered if Arment had been eavesdropping but would not ask an accusatory question. It didn't matter, anyway. Arment would hear about the previous night's incident through the town grapevine anyway.

What he wouldn't hear, Joseph promised himself, was that the newest hero of Dodge City let one misstep stop him cold. It looked like he would have to be a lawman for some time to come, like it or not. Pride left him no other option.

The rain swept in, hard and driving. The livery roof roared and snapped under the impact of sheets of falling water, then began to drip at numerous places.

"That's going to keep up for a good while," Arment said. "There goes a lot of our business for today, I guess. Uh, no trouble with Charlie Bassett, is there? I mean, nothing I'd need to know about . . . because of the livery, and you working for me, and all that?"

The very tone of Arment's question revealed his guilt. Joseph knew he'd eavesdropped. But it didn't much matter. "No, Caleb, nothing you'd need to know about. Just lawman business, that's all."

18

The rain fell for two hours, washing the roofs and walls of Dodge City clean and for a brief time purging the air of Dodge's usual conglomerate smell of cattle, smoke, and airborne dust. When the downpour ended, the smells began to return, but the mud generated by the storm lingered. It clung to Liam's boots as he trudged back to the livery and splattered the walls and boardwalks as wagons and buggies rolled past.

Liam had just left the office of an attorney whom he'd consulted not for legal advice but because he'd chanced to stumble upon a possible lead to Patrick Carrigan. Oddly, it had come about through an offhand comment by a waiter at a café who'd overheard Liam introducing himself to another man. "Carrigan?" the waiter had said. "Not all that common a name around here, but I did meet another Carrigan here once, sitting right where you are. A cattleman passing through who got himself into a row of some kind and had to get himself a lawyer to get out of it."

Liam had immediately pumped the man for information. Was it Patrick Carrigan? Why, yes, he thought it was. Who was the lawyer? That was Henry Taylor, who still had an office down the street.

Liam had finished his meal quickly, returned to the wagon works, and begged off work for a couple of hours. Something important had come up, he told Moore truthfully enough: He needed to pay a visit to an attorney's office. Moore was cooperative and gave Liam the time off. Liam headed straight for the law office of Henry Taylor.

It had been quite a worthwhile visit, and he could hardly wait to tell Joseph what he'd found. He gave a passing boy a quarter to go to the wagon works and tell Drake that an important matter had arisen and Liam would not be returning to work today.

He was musing over all this when a boy's voice reached him and caught his attention. The boy had just unleashed a string of expletives hot enough to set a dry forest on fire.

The source of the profanity was in a vacant lot to Liam's left. A second boy was with him, and together they were facing a third who was thin and several inches shorter than they.

"Hey, you little turd, I *ast*ed you a question!" the lead antagonist was saying, jabbing a finger toward his victim. "You talk to me when I ast you something!"

"Yeah!" echoed his partner. "You answer him that, turd!"

"Leave me alone!"

"Wrong answer!" The first boy's hand shot out and slapped the smaller boy's face, sharply enough so that the sound of the smack made Liam wince. The first boy's companion, an imitator rather than an initiator, tried to slap him, too, but missed. The first boy fired a disdainful glance at his partner but kept his attention on his victim.

"Leave me alone, you big ass!" the victimized boy said. He was trying to sound tough, but his voice quavered and gave him away.

"What did you call me?"

"Nothing. . . . Just leave me alone."

"He called you an ass, Billy," the second antagonist said.

In an instant, Billy had grabbed the smaller boy by the throat. "Take back what you said," he ordered.

The boy tried to talk but could only squeak.

"Take it back, turd! Take it back and say that it's you who's an ass."

The boy could barely get the words out of his constricted throat. "Let me . . . go. . . ." he gasped.

"Tell you what: I'll let you go as soon as you tell me where your daddy's face is. I hear it got blowed clean off in Tennessee!"

Liam felt his gut tighten. Good Lord . . . the victimized boy was a son of Mordecai Scott!

The smaller boy kicked and struggled.

"I mean, what the hell is he doing running around with a damned cloth on his face? My pap says it's because there ain't no face there. Says a good old Rebel blew it off because your pap is a sorry Yankee. Got what he deserved, Pap says. Too bad he didn't get his whole damn head blowed off! That's what my pap says. Know what he calls your pappy? Mashed-potato Face. Ha! You like that, you little turd? I ought to tear your face off so you can look like your ugly pap!"

The wiry victim struggled and fought for freedom, but his captor was too big and too strong. The second boy laughed at the show. They were all so distracted that they didn't notice Liam approaching them from the street, his face a storm cloud of fury.

Suddenly the Scott boy's anger gave him the strength to achieve a remarkable feat. He leaped up, letting his weight pull his throat free of the other boy's grasp. At the same time his right leg lashed out and kicked his antagonist in the belly.

Billy let out a great grunt and doubled over. The Scott boy hit the ground on his back but bounced right back up and was instantly upon Billy, fists and feet in a blur of motion. He fought not with skill but with spirit, and in the immediate situation, that gave him an advantage over Billy.

Liam stopped, recognizing that the boy had actually taken the situation into hand. Better to give him a few minutes of success before intervening.

The other boy with Billy seemed stunned, unwilling to fight but also too prideful to run away from a shrimp of a boy—even if the shrimp was at the moment getting the best of a whale. But when the boy looked up and saw Liam, he turned and ran away, leaving Billy to deal with the little whirlwind on his own.

The Scott boy could not prevail forever. Billy was simply too big and too strong, and after he got his wind back he managed to get a grip on his enemy and push him away. He was on his feet quickly, diving in on the Scott boy with such anger that there was a strong likelihood he would inflict serious injury.

It was time to intervene. Liam put a strong hand on Billy's shoulder and jerked him roughly back. Billy staggered backward on his heels, startled half to death because he hadn't even known that Liam was close by. The boy fell on his rump and stared up at Liam's tall, intimidating form. Liam stepped up, leaned over, and grabbed him by the chin.

"Son," he said in a low voice that was all the more threatening for that softness, "maybe you would like to find out firsthand what it's like to have no face. Would you?"

Billy sputtered and mumbled. Then he got to his feet

and ran away, casting a hateful glance back at the boy he'd antagonized and a look of fear at Liam.

"Are you all right, son?" Liam asked the Scott boy.

"Yes."

"Where are your parents?"

"They're at home."

"You're in town alone?"

"Yes. . . . I got to go, sir. Thank you for helping me." The boy wiped away a stray tear. He'd struggled hard not to cry but hadn't fully won the battle. Pride made him want to get away from human company so he could vent his tears without an audience.

"Your surname is Scott, I think. What's your first name?"

"I'm Timothy, sir. I got to go now."

"My name's Liam. Liam Carrigan. Why are you in town alone, Timothy?"

"Looking for my sister. I got to take her home. My ma is sick and she's wanted to see her for the longest time. I got to go now to find her, sir."

"Well, Timothy, I sure hope she's not as sick as that. Do your parents know you're here alone?"

Timothy did not answer. Instead he set off at a run, darting out of the lot, onto the street, and around the nearest corner.

Liam straightened his collar, headed back to the street, turned left, and went on to the livery to find Joseph. He felt oddly shaken; this interaction with young Timothy Scott was the most direct he'd had with the family of the man he'd mangled so many years ago.

It came to mind that in a small way he'd just done the very thing he felt called on to do: He'd helped out the Scott family, if only by breaking up a bit of bullying.

He slogged through the mud without any regard to its effect on his boots and trousers. He was eager to reach Joseph and tell him what he'd learned about Patrick Carrigan.

It looked as if there might be a halfway reasonable chance of finding their long-lost uncle after all.

Liam had expected an animated audience for his news, but Joseph disappointed him. He was distracted, dejected, more somber than Liam had seen him in months. Liam wanted to know why, and pressed the matter until Joseph relented, took him out into the alley and out of Arment's earshot, and told him about the incident in the saloon, the stabbed barkeep, and the visit from Bassett.

". . . And so Bassett went on his way and I went back inside the livery, and that was that. Arment had been eavesdropping. I can tell because he tried so hard to appear like he didn't know what we had been talking about."

Liam struggled to offer reassurance: "So you

balked a little, Joseph. Don't let it bother you too bad. It happens to the best lawmen, the best soldiers—all kinds of people. I can recall times during the war when I couldn't pull the trigger . . . couldn't have pulled it to save my own skin. Then, other times, you fight without any hesitation and do what you have to do."

"But it can't be that way for me, Liam. I was the law, the man people expected to solve the situation, and for a few seconds there I was as useless as a bull teat. If it had gone a couple of seconds longer, that barkeep would probably be dead."

Liam asked the undiplomatic but obvious question. "Any indications that what happened has damaged your standing among the local populace?"

"How could it not? People talk. Stories get spread, and what's bad in them is made out to be even worse. I'm worried something will even get into the newspaper."

"It's just something that happened. Nobody died. If you balked, it was only for a minute, and when you had to shoot, you did. So put it behind you."

"I'm ashamed of myself, Liam. I'll be honest about it and just admit it. One day I face down a whole gang, gun down men like I'm a dime-novel hero, and then the next time I freeze like Christmas just facing down one drunk with a pistol."

"Let it go."

Cameron Judd

Abruptly and surprisingly, Joseph chuckled. "Let it go, you say. Odd advice from a man who can't forget about one fight in a Tennessee farmhouse."

"Maybe you have a point. But speaking of that, I had an interesting little encounter this morning. I broke up a fight among a group of boys, one of them the son of Mordecai Scott."

Liam related the story. Joseph listened thoughtfully. "So he has a sister."

"Apparently." Liam paused, frowning as a new thought arose. "I'll be. I'll be."

"What?"

"I think I've found my opportunity to do something good for the Scott family."

"You're going to try to bring the sister back to the family, aren't you."

"I don't know why I didn't think of it earlier."

"You don't know her name."

"No."

"The boy may already have taken her back, Liam."

"Maybe. But maybe not. I can at least try to find out more about it all. It would be a good thing if I could bring a straying child back to her family."

"No denying that."

"Tell me something else, Joseph. What do you think of what I've found out about Uncle Patrick?"

"I think you've done fine. Sounds like we may be bound for Montana."

170

"But not right away. Not until I can do what I need to do."

"I'll tell you what I'll do, Liam: When I make my rounds tonight, I'll ask some questions. Maybe somebody will know who Scott's daughter is."

"I appreciate the help. But I want to be the one to take her home, if possible. It's me who owes good to the man, not you. No offense."

"None taken."

19

Joseph was true to his word, but his questions about Scott's daughter found no answers that night. Many people knew of Scott, whose habit of hiding his face behind a cloth had naturally made him a well-known figure. But about the daughter no one knew a thing, and soon Joseph stopped asking around about her.

He spent the evening traveling in and out of saloons, speaking to people, smiling, and playing the friendly, protective deputy marshal. But it seemed to him that people looked at him differently from the way they had right after he cleaned out the gang at the freight station. The story of his failure in the Long Branch was surely getting around.

He waited impatiently for his pocket watch to tick off the last minutes of his beat, thinking all the while about the information Liam had gleaned from the lawyer, and finding the thought of leaving town increasingly tempting.

* * *

Unknown to Joseph, Liam was also making the rounds of saloons and dance halls that night, but not for the reason he usually did. He was asking the same question as Joseph, trying vainly to find anyone who knew the daughter of Mordecai Scott. His results were no better than Joseph's. The strange figure of Mordecai Scott was known to almost all, but about his family in general and his daughter in particular, no one knew. It confirmed to Liam the degree to which Scott, and by extension his family, had lived a life cut off from society. All because of that terrible disfigurement. All because of Liam.

He understood in an intellectual way that what he had done to Mordecai Scott had been in the context of war—that he was, in a sense, not guilty. His heart told him otherwise. No matter what the context of the action, he was the one who had pulled the trigger of that shotgun and changed Scott's life forever.

Liam was still making the rounds, asking his questions, when Joseph returned to the room in the livery. Joseph wondered where his brother was and thought again of Mack Stanley. He hoped Stanley had moved on. If he had not, any dark corner or back alley was potentially a place from which Liam could be ambushed by the sneaking assassin.

Joseph's last thought before falling asleep was that he would indeed be glad to leave Dodge City behind.

* * *

Liam came in late, two thirty in the morning. Joseph did not awaken. Despite retiring at a later hour, Liam was the first to get up in the morning. He readied himself for work as usual, had his typical egg-and-biscuit breakfast with Joseph, and set off for the wagon works, riding his horse this time, not walking as he usually did.

Once there, though, he did not set to work as usual. Having already taken one afternoon away from work, he hated to ask Moore for this day as well. But there was an errand he had to run, he told his employer, and it couldn't wait.

Drake Moore was accommodating, as usual. Liam was given his day. He set off on his horse, westward.

Liam was quite nervous about what he was doing . . . if he knew what he was doing at all. This wasn't what he'd had in mind. His rather grandiose vision had involved a triumphant ride to the Scott homestead, bringing with him the straying daughter and the joy of a family reuniting.

It had seemed realistic and plausible the night before as he made his rounds. Now, in the light of day, it struck him as silly and unlikely. He'd not even been able to find out the girl's name. And even if he had, and had managed to track her down, who was he to think that he, a stranger, could persuade her to reconcile with her family? He didn't even know what had driven them apart in the first place.

So here he was, alone, riding along with a much less exalted ambition. Today he would locate the Scott home. Perhaps even make contact with the man. Maybe learn something about the situation, the missing daughter. Or find some other way to help out the man and his family.

Whenever he made contact, today or later, it would be clumsy. What could he say? "Hello, Mr. Scott . . . how you been? I'm the fellow who shot your face off and now I'm here to lend a helping hand. Got a shed needing painting?"

He wasn't sure at all how he'd handle the situation. But he was certain he was doing the right thing in trying.

The day was somewhat overcast, cooling the air but making Liam wonder if rain would come. If it did he'd be drenched; he'd not packed his poncho into his saddlebags.

Miles fell away. As he'd been told to do, he followed a wagon trail that cut first straight west, then north. The only problem was, there was more than one such trail, and he had no way to be sure he'd followed the correct one.

He forged ahead. The clouds grew thicker and the breeze cooler. Liam sighed. Too bad. It looked like he'd be getting wet after all.

According to the instructions he'd received, he should be nearing the place where Scott's sod house would be found. Assuming, of course, that he'd taken the right trail.

Inspiration hit him. If all this timed out correctly, the coming rain might give him a handy excuse for insinuating himself into the lives of the Scotts. He could ask for shelter in their home, strike up acquaintance—no talk of his war history, obviously—and from there seek to build a friendship that would allow him to help the family out.

Liam spotted a sod house just as the clouds grew twice as dark within a five-minute span. Probably not Scott's place—the odds of finding it right away struck him as unlikely—but he still rode toward it with heart pounding, because one could never know, and sometimes the unlikely happened.

The man who appeared at the door wasn't Scott. He was a slovenly, fat, unkempt fellow wearing filthy canvas pants and a shirt with the sleeves cut off at the armpits. He had a shotgun and watched Liam with squinting eyes.

"Far enough. . . . Are you friend or foe?"

Friend or foe? An odd question. "I'm a friend," Liam answered. "Just a rider hoping to use your shed there to wait out the rain, if that's agreeable to you."

"You ain't sent by the sheriff, are you?"

"No."

"You better not be. . . . I ain't afraid to use this shot-gun. If she's been talking about me again, I guaran-damn-tee you ain't a word of it true!"

Liam touched the brim of his hat. "I'm not a law-man, but if you're that worried about it, I'll be moving on. I've got no ambition to get shot today."

Liam turned his horse and began to ride away. The rain began to fall.

"Hold up there, friend," the man said. "No reason to be riding in the rain. Put your horse in the shed and come on in. I've got a bit of whiskey I'll share."

"Cordial of you," Liam said as he headed his horse toward the shed. He wondered if he was doing the right thing. This man didn't seem to have the machinery between his ears in good working order. But this was going to be a hard rain, and whiskey would go down well just now, even if it was early.

The man had leaned the shotgun up against one of the dirt walls. He eyed Liam closely. "You sure you ain't law?"

"I'm not. My job's at the wagon shop. But I've got a brother who's a deputy marshal."

The man pondered a moment or two, then bright-ened like dawn. "Hang my granny—you ain't brother to the one who gunned down them thieves at the freight house, are you?"

"I am."

"Well! You get *two* drinks of whiskey for that!"

"So I'm getting rewarded for being brother to a lawman? I didn't think you liked lawmen."

"I don't. But only when they're bothering me. If they get thieves and robbers and such, I'm right there with them."

"Can I ask what the law would be after you for? You ain't dangerous, are you?"

"Why, I'm as gentle a little kitten as you'll find. Roll a ball of twine acrost the floor and I'll chase it. Scratch behind my ear and I'll purr."

"I'll just take your word for that."

"That sorry harlot of a woman of mine, though, she gets mad at me sometimes and goes off to town for a month or so and tells tales that I beat on her and steal cattle and set folks' barns afire. All lies. But the sheriff has come calling a time or two, just to get her off his back, you know. Once some fool deputy actually hauled me in and throwed me right in the calaboose for burning down a barn. Hell, the barn wasn't even burned. It's still standing! The deputy was just a young fool, that's all. He didn't last."

"I'm Liam Carrigan, by the way."

"Josiah Poohter, with a 'h' in the middle. Never leave out the 'h.' Pleased to know you."

Judging from the man's general smell, Poohter was a remarkably appropriate last name, but Liam didn't voice that observation. His host had been moving about, scrounging up a crockery bottle of whiskey and a couple of cracked coffee cups all the while he'd been talking. He poured Liam a generous shot and handed him the cup. Liam observed the crust around most of the rim and turned the cup until he could find a relatively clean sipping point.

Poohter drank his in two swallows. Liam sipped, mostly to keep the whiskey from making contact with the crust on the side of the cup.

"Tell me the news from Dodge," Poohter said. "I ain't been to town for a spell."

Liam shared what news he could. Poohter really wanted to hear the true details of Joseph's heroism at the freight station. He'd heard only a garbled version so far, from a passing man who had Joseph all but gunning down an entire army with his left hand while rescuing a distressed damsel with his right.

Even without embellishment, though, Joseph's story was a notable one, and Poohter was duly impressed. He poured Liam a second shot of whiskey, but Liam decided he'd secretly pour out some of it. He didn't want to drink too much and smell of liquor when he found the Scotts.

Poohter was busy telling stories of other incidents of violent law enforcement involving the Masterson brothers, Wyatt Earp, and others of Dodge City fame. Liam only half listened. The rain was coming down hard, and he wondered how much would have to fall before a sod house got so wet that it gave way. A lot, he supposed. This place looked solid enough, and not a drop was coming through anywhere, other than some puddling at the base of the open door.

Liam waited until Poohter's storytelling waned, then said, "Hey, let me ask you something. They tell me there's a man who lives out here somewhere who wears a cloth because he got his face pretty much shot away when he was robbing a bank back east somewhere. Is that true?"

"Oh, there's a man who wears a mask, that's true, and his face is shot all to hell, but it didn't happen during no bank robbery. Worse than that. It happened when the sorry bastard fought for the bluebellies. And I say here's to it." He raised his mug as if in toast, then drank the final drops of his whiskey. "I just wish it had kilt him. Him and every other sorry bluebelly who ever crawled. I hate 'em all."

"I take it you were a good defender of the rights of the states," Liam said.

"You, too, I hope. For if not, you're not welcome in this house."

Even if Liam hadn't really been a Confederate, he would be now, talking to this militant. "I fought for the Stars and Bars, just like you."

Poohter liked that. A big grin split his homely face. More whiskey poured. A toast to the Confederacy. Liam took only the tiniest sip, then poured out most of the drink when Poohter wasn't looking.

"So does this no-face man live around here?"

"Somewhere within ten, fifteen miles of here. I don't know just where and I don't care where, as long as he keeps his damn self and his brood away from me. I got no use for a Yank."

"All the same, kind of got to feel sorry for a man who has suffered what he did," Liam ventured.

"Ha! I don't feel sorry for him. I just wish whoever had shot him had blowed his brains out instead of just messing up his face."

"You know, I wouldn't mind taking a look at a man like that. Just to see what it looks like, you know."

Poohter thought about that a moment, then his eyes narrowed and gleamed. He began to chuckle and grow red-faced. "I'd like to find him and steal his mask and run him to town and dump him out! He'd be running around all squalling and trying to hide that ugly head any way he could! Haw! That'd be a sight!"

Any initial liking Liam might have felt for his strange host vanished. Poohter had just suggested something unforgivably cruel. No wonder his woman wouldn't stay with him.

"Well, I do feel sorry for the man," Liam said. "I'd just like to get a look at him, that's all. You don't know where he lives, do you?"

"No. I reckon that Stump might know."

"Who's Stump?"

"Runs himself a whiskey drinking house up about

two mile from here, yonder way." He pointed toward the northwest. "He knows where everybody lives."

Liam nodded. He'd make a call on Stump as soon as the rain let up and he could get there.

Poohter started talking again, this time about buffalo hunting, which he'd done in the earliest days of this region, when Dodge was known as a center for that trade rather than as a cattle town. Liam listened as best he could; every now and then something Poohter said sparked in him a moment of real interest, but for the most part he watched the rain and counted the minutes until he could leave. Poohter offered him food, but Liam, who in his time had eaten grubby food spiced with battlefield mud—son-of-a-bitch stew served with rattlesnake meat included on purpose and bugs included by accident—wasn't about to dine on any fare Poohter could offer.

The rain stopped and Liam made a quick exit. Poohter actually seemed sorry to see him go. Probably it was very lonely out there, especially when his woman had run off to Dodge again.

20

Despite the apparent flatness of the landscape, there were in fact many rises and falls in elevation, like hills that had been mashed nearly flat by the foot of God so that their bases were widened vastly and their height diminished until they were nearly imperceptible.

Liam rode over the crest of one such elevation and saw below him, in all its splendor, the fine establishment whose sign proclaimed it to be the Stumptown Saloon. Around it was a sort of an excuse for a community: a poorly made log house constructed out of logs far too twisted and gnarled for that purpose, one shack made out of real sawed lumber, and several sod dwellings. The saloon appeared to be the centerpiece of the community. As Liam rode down toward it he wondered if Stump was called Stump because he ran a saloon in Stumptown, or if he was the leading citizen and the settlement was named after him. Maybe he was the one who lived in the shack made from real lumber.

He was nearly to the saloon when he saw the man who had to be Stump. He walked out of the saloon door with a pot of something in his hand, then tossed it onto the ground to the delight of a band of mangy curs that hung around the place and had already been barking to announce Liam's approach. Stump had to move his legs a lot when he stood still, for he kept teetering and tilting one way or the other when he wasn't in motion, and had to always be catching himself. The reason was that his legs were made of wood from the knees down, sailor-style peg legs attached with straps.

Stump looked up at Liam as he rode down the shallow decline. Liam nodded a greeting but Stump didn't return it. By the time Liam was hitching his horse outside the saloon, Stump was back inside behind the bar, immersing in a big tub of water the stew pot he'd just emptied.

There were three men already in the saloon, two playing cards in one corner, another leaned back against a wall in the opposite corner, a hat covering his face and a slicker covering his body. He was breathing in the slow, steady pattern of a man deeply sleeping.

"What for you?" Stump growled from behind the bar.

"How's your beer?"

"Wet, warm, and stale."

"That'll do."

Stump, who seemed a grouchy soul, grunted something beneath his breath and pulled a mug from a shelf. He filled it with beer that had little head and few bubbles, and put it before Liam.

Liam wasn't really interested in beer, especially after a sip revealed that Stump had been very accurate in his description. He was there to find out how to locate Scott's dwelling, but given the reaction he'd received on the subject from Poohter, he wanted to feel out the situation before he brought up the matter here.

He'd hoped to find Stump to be one of those talkative, informative barmen, but he wasn't. He was sullen and quiet and wore a perpetual grimace. However, it was amazing to watch him move around and keep himself upright on those two sticks he walked on.

"Do you serve food here?" Liam asked as he took a second swallow of stale beer.

"Serve stew. You're too late, though: I done give it to the dogs. It was going bad. You'd not have wanted it."

"If you've got bread and butter, that would do for me. Just something to fill the belly."

"I got bread. Butter, no. Got some grease if you want to use that."

"Bread alone's fine."

The bread was as stale as the beer, but when taken together each moderated the other. Liam ate and sipped and eyed the two cardplayers. Every now and then the man sleeping under his hat on the other side of the room would shift a little, rumble and sputter, then fall into a soft snore.

"I'm looking for somebody," Liam said to Stump when it became obvious no conversation would be forthcoming from the other side without prodding.

"Don't know 'em," Stump said.

"I didn't say who I was looking for."

"I don't give aid to lawmen or bounty hunters or no one seeking to cause problems for somebody else, especially when the problems ain't none of my business."

"You make a lot of assumptions, Mr. Stump. I'm not wanting to cause trouble. I want to give a hand to a fellow who I think could use it."

"Who?"

"Last name is Scott. I don't know the first. He had a bad injury to his face during the war, and wears a mask to keep it covered."

To Liam's surprise, Stump's sour expression softened. He clumped over to stand across from Liam on the other side of the bar, hanging on to it to maintain his balance.

"Mordecai Scott. I know who you're talking about. Poor fellow. I pity him."

"I do too," Liam replied. He decided to tell as much of the truth as he felt he could get by with. "In fact, I want to lend him a hand, do some work for him, help him out in some way. I saw him in Dodge and heard what happened to him. It so happens I saw a man injured in just the same way during the war. I've always remembered that, and I think it's the thing to do to help out Mr. Scott."

Stump seemed suspicious. Liam didn't blame him. He doubted many of the people who came to this outlying waterhole were the sort to be looking for ways to aid their fellow man.

"I happen to like Mr. Scott," Stump said. "I feel a bit of kinship with him, having some wartime memories of my own." He glanced down toward his wooden pegs. "I wouldn't want to play a part in seeing harm done to him."

"Why would anyone want to harm him?"

"Some folks don't require much reason. I've seen that man mistreated more times than I can count. He was in here a few times . . . finally quit coming because folks either treated him like he was the devil or like he was something to be laughed at or made fun of. There was a whore-girl once, from out of Dodge, who come in here when Mordecai was having a drink over in yonder corner where that man is sleeping. Somebody thought it would be funny to have her pull off his cloth. She did. Screamed and fainted, that girl did. And I don't much blame her. I never seen a human face so mangled up. There ain't much there."

"I know. I caught a glimpse in Dodge."

"It ain't the thing to do to ask folks their names, but in this case I'd like to know yours."

"My name's Liam Carrigan."

"Carrigan? Why, hell, you *are* a lawman! You're the one that shot up that gang in Dodge the other day. Everybody that come in here talked about that for days. Get on with you. I ain't putting the law onto a man who's been struck hard enough by bad luck. Pshaw!" Stump waved dismissively at Liam and began to turn away.

"Wait, Mr. Stump. That wasn't me: That was my brother, Joseph. He's the lawman, not me."

"You help him, though. Bound to, him being your brother. That's been the way with them sorry Mastersons, brother helping brother. What? Did your brother send you out to arrest him for something or other?"

"No. I swear, I came on my own, for my own reasons."

"Why do you really want to see Mordecai Scott?"

Liam paused. "Because that time I saw a man shot and mangled in the same way . . . it was me who pulled the trigger of the shotgun. I've felt bad about it ever since."

Stump worked his jaws while evaluating Liam, his chin moving from side to side, almost as if he were chewing. He nodded. "I'm going to trust you, Mr. Carrigan. I'll draw you a map to show you how to reach Mordecai Scott's place. But if I hear that he's been mistreated or arrested or anything at all like that, I won't forget you, and next time I see you I'll be on you with a sawed-off Greener. And I mean that."

Stump seemed the kind to be taken seriously. "I believe you. No harm is going to come to him from me, I assure you."

"One more question: You ain't coming out here for no reason to do with his daughter, are you?"

"I know he has a daughter, but I don't know who she is. No, it has nothing to do with her."

"You don't know her? She's in Dodge."

"I don't know her. I've only been in Dodge a brief time."

"Are you a whoring man? Because she's a whore. She run off from home and broke her folks' hearts. Turned whore in Dodge City."

"I don't know her."

"Broke her folks' hearts," Stump repeated. "Aye, Lawd—what is it about folks that makes them go do such things? Deborah is as pretty a peach as ever growed in the orchard, and there she went and turned whore. Her poor mama, my goodness, how it hurt her poor mama. And Mordecai too."

"Why'd she do it?"

"Story is, she was ashamed of her father so much, his face and the mask and all, and the way other young folks would point and laugh and treat her bad because of it, that she just turned on her folks and run off. I don't know if that's all there was to it or not. I know they try to get her to come home, but she won't."

"Will you help me out, Mr. Stump?" he asked.

"I'll help you. And my last name's Perkins. Not Stump, so stop this 'Mr. Stump' nonsense. Stump's just my nickname."

"Because of losing your legs in the war."

"Hell, no! My pap called me that when I was a boy, because I was so dang short."

"Sorry."

Stump laughed. It was odd to see that grouchy-looking face smile. "Just funning you! Of course it's because of the legs. Lemme see . . . where's that pencil stub?"

Stump poked around under the bar and came out with a piece of paper and a pencil. He drew a map and went over it quickly with Liam.

Liam was glad to have the map. He'd be able to find the Scott place with relative ease. But he'd already decided not to go there right away, not now that he had a name to connect with the straying daughter: Deborah Scott. He'd go back to Dodge and ask more questions. Armed with her name, surely he'd be able to find her. Whether he could persuade her to come back to her family was a whole other matter, but it couldn't hurt to try.

Liam paid his bill, plus extra for the help, and walked out of the grubby little saloon. The two cardplayers in the corner were still at it, but the man who had been sleeping in the corner had quit snoring a few minutes back, precisely at the moment Liam had introduced himself. Neither Liam nor Stump had noticed.

He rose and headed out the door. Liam was riding away, back toward Dodge. The man unhitched his own horse, swung into the saddle, and rode off in the same direction Liam had, but not precisely on his trail. He kept off to the side and far enough back so as not to be immediately picked out by Liam should he look back.

The two riders, spaced widely apart, rode northeastward away from Stumptown, out onto the rolling plains.

21

The shot came from a distance, and even before he heard the crack of it Liam knew he was being fired at, because his horse gave a strange shudder and spasm, keeled to the right, stumbling, and pitched over, dumping him out of the saddle and pinning his leg to the ground beneath the dying animal's weight.

A fountain of blood spewed from a hole in the horse's neck. The bullet had penetrated some major vein or artery. The creature's eyes were wide and wild, its legs twitched spasmodically, and it made terrible sounds of suffering and shock.

Liam was in pain himself, trapped by his own fallen mount, and was so surprised by what had happened that everything around him seemed to have taken on an unreal quality.

There was no more immediate gunfire. The angle of Liam's fall had put the horse between him and his would-be assassin. Right now the shooter was probably circling around to find a clear angle to allow a fatal shot. Liam had to get free quickly.

But he couldn't. The horse was too heavy, and Liam's ankle felt crushed. Soon, he feared, his leg would grow numb, the circulation pinched off by the horse's weight. It wouldn't matter much if his assailant found a better position: Liam would be a dead man.

He pitied his doomed horse. Life was flowing out of the bullet wound in gouts with every beat of its heart. The geysers of blood had subsided as the animal weakened.

Liam managed to get his pistol out. With his heart breaking, he put the muzzle against the horse's head. He was just about to pull the trigger and send a merciful bullet into its brain when the horse gave a great shudder and tried to rise. It was inevitably a failed effort, but its motion gave Liam just enough freedom from the horse's crushing weight to pull his leg free and roll out of the way before the horse's dead weight could collapse back onto him again.

Liam sucked in air for a few moments, his ankle throbbing. But the pain began to lessen, and he returned his attention to what he'd been about to do.

He put the pistol to the horse's head and pulled the trigger. Death was instantaneous—not even a twitch or a whinny.

With that done, Liam realized there was no hope of

getting the saddle off without help, but there was no time for that anyway. Somebody out there had just tried to kill him.

Or maybe not. Maybe it was a hunter, a stray shot. Such things happened.

Liam knelt behind his fallen horse and managed to work his rifle out of the boot. He felt better now with a weapon that had some distance. He dug ammunition out of the saddlebag that wasn't under the horse—thank heaven he'd put it in that one rather than the other—and dropped it into his pocket. Armed and no longer pinned down, he looked for cover. A small creek flowed about two hundred yards to his rear. He ran for it. The bank, though low, would give some cover. The trees as well.

Any hope that the shot that had killed his horse had been accidental was erased when another bullet sang past a split second before the sound of the shot reached him. It was high and wide, but even so, being shot at was a sobering thing. It made Liam's mind flash back to battlefields full of smoke, fire, and blood; it reminded him of the times he'd listened to the singing of minié balls past his head while men around him grunted and fell.

Liam ran as well as his hurting ankle and tingling leg would let him, and dropped down onto his belly at the edge of the creek. The bank shielded him from view from almost anywhere in the surrounding area. He slid along through the dirt and mud until he reached a clump of cottonwoods right at the edge of the creek. There he was almost entirely protected. He scanned the horizon but saw nothing. Then he pulled himself to a seated position and began to examine his ankle and gingerly rub his leg.

No broken bones and the pain was decreasing. He'd come out lucky on that one.

Who might have shot at him? He could think of only one person who had a reason to do so. That person had done this very thing once before, during the dismal cattle drive up from Texas.

But how had Mack Stanley found him all the way out there? Then Liam remembered the man sleeping in Stump's place, his face hidden. Maybe Liam had found Mack Stanley rather than the other way around.

After ten minutes Liam ventured another look around. He rose slightly, staying behind the tree, and tried to spot signs of movement.

He saw no one. Whoever had shot at him, whether Stanley or somebody else, had probably moved on. He hoped so.

Liam ventured a step from behind the tree.

The bullet burned like a heated iron as it ripped through the flesh of his leg. Liam went down like a tenpin, knocking the breath from his lungs. He lay still, his leg on fire, his lungs unable to draw wind, face flat in the mud. Rolling, he returned to his safe spot, still trying to breathe. His lungs kicked in and he sucked air.

The burning in his leg began to turn to a throb.

He was bleeding fairly heavily, but as he tore a slit in his trousers and managed to wipe away some of the blood, he saw that the wound was shallow, just a furrow cut through skin and muscle on the outer part of his left thigh. Thank God! The pain had been sufficient to make him fear that he might have suffered major damage.

With strips torn from his shirt and the application of pressure, he was eventually able to stanch the bleeding. Then he did his best to forget the wound and keep his attention focused on the landscape around him.

Liam was able to position himself so that his back and right side were completely shielded by cottonwoods, leaving him to worry only about the areas in front of him and to his left. He considered the latter the more vulnerable of the two and scanned the area back and forth.

There! He'd just seen a man scrambling across toward a jumble of boulders, rifle in hand. He could make out nothing of his features—could hardly even tell the color of his clothing—but there was no doubt he'd just seen his assailant.

He raised his rifle and fired three quick shots in the general direction of the man he'd seen. A shot in response struck the cottonwood not a yard from Liam's head.

Liam flattened himself on the ground and decided

that his best hope was to avoid offensive action. Keep sharp, keep low, and respond if need be, but if not, keep still. Eventually night would fall and he would be able to escape.

Hours passed; they felt like days. Liam saw occasional movement in the area of the rocky tangle, erasing more than once his hope that the man had grown tired of it all and moved on. The fact that he hadn't was quite worrisome, for it showed dedication. Whoever this was was serious about doing him in.

Liam realized that his enemy was waiting for darkness too. He probably planned to use it for cover, to move in invisibly and attack at point-blank range.

Escape would be a matter of timing his run, of moving out before the other man moved in. Either that, or it would be the luck of the shootout. Liam wanted to avoid that.

It came to mind that he might have a bit of trouble running, considering that his ankle still hurt. Maybe the assassin out there knew that and was banking on it.

Time rolled on, making him restless. Liam watched the sun crawl across the sky. He looked down the creek and wondered if there might be any route of hidden escape. There was not.

Four hours after he'd taken to his hiding place, he saw movement in the rocks again. It seemed to him that when he looked between two of the rocks very carefully, he could make out what appeared to be something white in motion. It could well be a white shirt. Carefully he took aim and squeezed the trigger slowly. . . .

When the smoke from his shot had cleared, he looked at the space between the rocks. Nothing white moved there now. Maybe he'd hit the fellow. There was no way to know without investigation, and he wasn't going to risk that yet.

Liam hoped he'd hit his assailant, especially if it was Mack Stanley. That man had tried to kill him one time too many.

Liam resettled himself, screwed up his patience, and watched the sun tick off the minutes across the sky.

Dusk had just begun to fall when Liam heard the rattle of a wagon. It was coming up the trail that ran between him and the rocks where his attacker had hidden. He lifted his head and looked, hopeful that this would be a source of help.

It was Mordecai Scott. He was perched on the wagon with his son Timothy beside him. There was no one else with them. Scott was wearing his mask, but it was rolled up so that his face was uncovered. Liam gazed at the mangled mass of scar tissue and the empty left eye socket, horrible even in the dusk, across some distance.

The wagon stopped abruptly. Scott said something to his son, who hopped down and ran right over toward the rocks where the gunman was hiding.

It all happened so fast that Liam was caught by surprise and failed to shout a warning, but when the boy went right behind the rocks without hesitation, and did not either raise a shout himself or come rushing back again, Liam realized the situation must have changed. A few moments later the boy reemerged, hitching his trousers. Obviously his father had stopped to let him relieve himself behind the rocks.

It was equally obvious that there was no one, living or dead, behind the rocks any longer, or the boy wouldn't have nonchalantly relieved himself. So if Liam's last shot had hit the man at all, it must not have been fatal, but it must have been sufficient to drive him away.

Liam noticed now that the boy was speaking to his father, gesturing back toward the rocks. Scott climbed down from the wagon and went with his son in that direction.

This was the best time to emerge. Liam opted to leave his weapons behind so as not to startle them.

Father and son were still behind the rocks, kneeling and looking at something and talking, when Liam came out onto the road. His ankle hurt and his leg was bloody, but the blood was crusted now and there was no fresh bleeding.

"Hello!" Liam called. "Is there someone here who can help me?"

Scott emerged from behind the rocks, pulling down his mask.

"Who are you?" Scott called. His voice had a somewhat distorted quality, probably a result of the physical damage to his face and mouth.

"My name's Carrigan, Liam Carrigan," Liam said to the man whom he'd thought for years that he'd killed. "I'm afraid I've been shot."

"By who?"

"I don't know. Somebody shot at me while I was riding. See my dead horse yonder? The first shot hit my horse and mortally wounded it. I had to mercy shoot it. Another bullet got me in the leg, but I shot back and thought I might have hit the man behind the rocks."

Scott was looking at the dead horse, which he evidently had not noticed until Liam pointed it out. He glanced over at Liam, who met his eye. "Never mind this cloth I wear," he said. "I suffered a face injury during the war and wear it to cover up the damage." He said it with the practiced tone of a man who'd been saying those same lines for many years. "I think you did hit whoever was back there, sir. There's blood. My boy noticed it when he went back there to pee."

"Can I approach you? I left my guns back yonder in those cottonwoods."

"Come on, then. But slow. I trust you, but I do have a pistol on me."

He did. It was holstered backward on his right hip. He was a left-hander, evidently. Liam felt a chill come rushing back to him after years of being forgotten: During that hand-to-hand fight in the farmhouse, his enemy had used his left hand more than his right. Liam had noticed it because it affected the way he had to fend him off. He now surrendered any lingering doubt that Scott and that unfortunate soldier were one and the same man.

Scott looked at Liam through the eyehole of the cloth. It had only one, Scott having one good eye.

Scott thrust out his hand. "I'm Mordecai Scott," he said. "I hope the cloth don't disturb you. It disturbs people worse when I don't wear it."

"It's fine. Does it get hot, wearing that?"

"Sometimes. When I'm alone or at home, where there's only the family around, I don't wear it. They're used to seeing me."

"I don't mind if you want to take it off."

"I'll leave it on. How bad hurt are you?"

"Not bad. Took a pretty good furrow through the leg, and it bled a lot, as you can see. And when my horse fell it hurt my ankle some, but again, nothing bad. I was lucky."

"I reckon so. By the way, that's my son Timothy yonder."

"Hello, young man," Liam said. "Remember me?"

Timothy nodded shyly and looked away.

"You know my son?" Scott asked in surprise.

"Timothy and I ran across each other in town," Liam said. He didn't want to say more than that: It might embarrass Timothy for his father to hear how he was picked on and mocked because of his father's appearance. Liam figured something out: Scott must have gone to Dodge to fetch back his son. Timothy must have failed to find his sister. There was no one else in the wagon.

Timothy turned his back on Liam, eyeing him for a moment over his shoulder and tugging on his father's arm to make him stoop down so that Timothy could whisper to him.

Scott stood. "Timothy tells me you drove off some bullies who were giving him a problem."

"All I did was help. He'd already torn into the worse of the pair like a whirlwind. Very impressive young fellow he is."

"Thank you for helping him. My children . . . they have suffered much because of my appearance, you see. People mock at me, and the children get some of the same just because they are my children. It can be a cruel world, sir, and not at all fair. I appreciate anyone who stands up for my children. Thank you."

Scott seemed honestly moved, and that in turn moved Liam. "It was not that big a thing . . . just busting up a little bit of boyish troublemaking."

"Why were you shot at?" Scott asked.

"I think I know who did it. I believe it was a man named Mack Stanley, who recently worked for me and my brother when we were running a herd of longhorns up from Texas. Along the way I caught him trying to steal a pistol belonging to my brother. We gave him a second chance, but he'd taken such a dislike to me that he took a shot at me from hiding. We sent him packing. He tried to kill me again in Dodge. And I think he tried a third time today."

"Listen, Mr. Carrigan, would you come with Timothy and me to our house? I'll get my wife to look over that wound and bind up your ankle. Then we can see to getting your dead horse dealt with, and your saddle and so on removed. I'll be glad to haul it all back to Dodge for you, and I can take you in, too, if you don't mind waiting until tomorrow. I'd like to do something for the man who helped my son." Scott tousled his son's hair. "The boy shouldn't have run off to Dodge like he did. He does that from time to time. Trying to find his sister and bring her home."

"I appreciate the invitation, but I hate to put you out."

"You're not putting us out. We don't get many guests. Folks are kind of skittish of a man with a face like mine."

Liam wasn't prepared for the great flood of guilt that that comment aroused. Scott, clearly a kindhearted and neighborly sort, had the face that he did because of Liam Carrigan. Never mind that it had happened in war, and never mind that in that fight Scott probably would have shot away Liam's face as quickly as Liam had shot away his. Those were hypotheticals. The reality was that it was Scott who had suffered, and Liam who had caused it.

"I'd be honored to be your guest, sir."

"Glad to have you. Sorry again about the mask."

"You don't need to keep saying that. I don't mind it, and don't mind if you take it off."

Timothy looked up at Liam. "It embarrasses him that he has to wear it," he said softly. "But it embarrasses him worse if he don't."

For a moment it was all Liam could do to keep from breaking out in tears and crying like a child.

22

As Liam limped into the sod house on the heels of Mordecai Scott, the first thought he had was that it was difficult to blame Deborah Scott for having cleared out of that place. How a family of two parents and three children had ever lived there was hard to imagine. The quarters were close, the house rather oppressive and dark. But it was as neat and clean as a house made out of dirt could be.

Scott's wife was named Laurel. She was evidently not feeling well, coughing a lot and looking haggard and pale. She seemed as happy to see Timothy as she was surprised to have a visitor. She scolded Timothy for having run off to town, but hugged rather than punished him.

She looked at Liam a little suspiciously but was cordial enough in her own quiet way. Supper was cooking on an iron stove: Beans bubbled in a pot while cornbread baked in a Dutch oven.

The other son was named Leroy. He seemed a little more shy than Timothy. Liam glanced around, looking for a family portrait that might show the daughter's face, but there were no portraits. The Scotts could not afford the services of photographers.

Laurel Scott cleaned and bandaged Liam's wounds and used rags to bind his ankle, which greatly reduced his limp. Then she served a supper that was plain but delicious, and Liam reflected that not all the fortunes of Mordecai Scott had been bad ones. He had a good family and a truly wonderful wife. And if Liam was successful, perhaps he'd have his straying daughter back again too.

"I've seen you before," Liam said to Scott at the end of the meal. "You were at the wagon works sometime back. I saw you there."

"I was there. I don't recall seeing you, though."

"You probably didn't see me. I was inside the building while you were in the back. I work there now, by the way."

"Do you? Well, that's a good place. Mr. Moore has always been fair with me, and does good work."

"I've learned a lot from him."

"Why aren't you working today?"

"I needed the day off to come out here . . . looking for my friend, a fellow named Arrowood."

"Do you think this man who shot at you followed you from Dodge?"

"I think it's more likely that he was in a saloon I stopped at a few miles from here."

"Stump's business."

"Yes. There was a man in there sleeping with his face covered up. It was probably Mack Stanley. I believe he followed me from there."

"Do you think he's actually hunting you?"

"I think he saw an opportunity and decided to take it. I don't know what will happen now. Maybe he'll leave me be, or maybe he'll be after me until he has a chance to gun me down. He's tried three times now to get me."

"You should go to the law."

"That should be easy enough. My brother is a deputy marshal in Dodge."

"Carrigan . . ." Scott paused. "I'll be! Is he the one who wiped out that army of outlaws at the freight station?"

"It wasn't quite an army, but yes, that was him."

"He must be quite a fighter."

"I reckon he is. I never thought of him that way, but after what he did, there's no denying it: He's a good fighter."

Timothy spoke up. "My father was a good fighter once. Back during the war."

"I guess I wasn't good enough," Scott said, touching the mask.

"He was shot with buckshot," Timothy said. "That's what happened to him."

"Hush up, son," Laurel said. "Your pap doesn't like talking about that."

Liam winked at Timothy. "You're a good fighter yourself, Timothy. You had that bully thrashing for his life for a spell there in that empty lot."

Laurel Scott didn't look too happy at seeing her son praised for fighting, but Liam had the oddest sense that Mordecai Scott had smiled.

"I hate Billy," Timothy said. "I'd like to kill him, I swear."

"Tim!" his mother declared in a tone of shock.

"I do hate him, Ma. He's mean."

"Son, you have to learn to let things go," Mordecai said. "I know all about meanness. I encounter it everywhere I go. If I hated everyone who did something bad to me, I'd spend my life angry and raging. You got to learn to forgive people."

"Even when they don't deserve it?"

"Son, the whole point of forgiving is that they don't deserve it."

Liam wondered if his face revealed any of the guilt that was overwhelming him at that moment.

"I'm surprised Stump didn't tell you that this man Arrowood you were looking for didn't live in these parts," Scott said to Liam. "He knows everybody for miles around."

"I didn't ask him," Liam said. "I guess I should have. But as things have fallen out, I've at least had the pleasure of your hospitality. Fine family you have here. Two good sons. You can't ask more than that."

Timothy, evidently the family member with the least control over his tongue, spoke right up as Liam had hoped he would. "There's Deborah, too, but she ain't here. I tried to bring her home, but I couldn't find her."

"Thank God you couldn't, considering the places she goes and the things she does," Laurel said in a bitter tone.

"Now, honey," Mordecai Scott said, "there's no call to talk so."

"I just wish she'd . . ." Remembering their visitor, she did not finish whatever she was going to say.

Scott peered at Liam through the hole in the cloth; it looked so strange that Liam honestly wished he'd just remove the mask. "Our daughter is wayward," he said. "She's hurt her mother, and me, by the way she's gone. I don't know exactly why she did it. I've always felt it had something to do with living with constant shame over how I look and how I tend to isolate myself from folks because of it. Somehow it just drove her to turn her back on her family and go down some very wicked paths."

"I didn't mean to bring up a hurtful matter," Liam said.

"You couldn't know."

He had known, of course—part of it, anyway—but there was no call to share that with the family.

"Every now and again, especially when Laurel is feeling poorly, our boy Timothy there gets the notion he'll go into Dodge to find his sister and bring her back," Scott said. "He walks all the way by himself. Usually we notice it and bring him back before he gets far. This time he made it all the way to Dodge. I had to look for him a long time to find him."

"That's quite a walk. Do you know for certain that Deborah lives in Dodge?"

Scott looked down. "A lot of the time. Sometimes she goes off to other towns, so nobody knows where she is. There's times that for weeks at a stretch she has gone home with . . . To tell the truth, I'd as soon not talk about it. It's not easy to confess to someone that your daughter has made a harlot of herself, but it's the cold fact."

"She ought to be proud of you, sir. You seem a good father and a good man, from all I can see."

"Thank you. But how can you be proud of a man who has to hide his own ugliness?"

"We're proud of you, Pa," Leroy contributed. "Me and Tim and Mama, we're proud."

Mordecai nodded under the mask.

Liam decided to be bold. "Sir, I wish you'd take off the mask. You needn't hide from me. To be honest, I already saw beneath it when you were at the wagon shop, and today when you rode in on the wagon. Go ahead. You needn't wear that thing in your own home."

Scott slowly reached up, hesitated, then took off the mask.

Even though he had caught glimpses of Scott's disfigurement before, this was the first truly close and clear look that Liam had gotten of the damage he'd done to this man all those years before. He did his best to maintain an expressionless face, but he was sure his shock showed through.

"I'm sorry if it bothers you to see it," Mordecai said.

"Nothing to be sorry for," Liam said. "I'm pleased you decided not to hide from me."

Conversation waned. There was no dessert in so poor a household, but Laurel boiled coffee and that served as a good substitute. As time went by and Liam became accustomed to Mordecai's shocking appearance, he found that it bothered him less and less to look at him.

Maybe, if he'd not hidden his face so much over the years, Mordecai might have been able to find community acceptance. People had the ability to grow used to things, and there were plenty of disfigured people since the war.

It struck him that maybe the worst damage he'd done to Mordecai Scott in the farmhouse that day hadn't been to his face but to his self-respect. And that seemed to Liam the saddest thought he'd had in a long time.

* * *

The next afternoon Mordecai's wagon rolled to the edge of Dodge and stopped. He was wearing his mask again, for he'd entered busier climes, where there were more people to stare, point, maybe laugh or express horror.

"If you don't care, this is as far as I'll take you," he said to Liam. "I try to stay out of town if I can. I don't take much to seeing people, you know."

"This is fine." Liam climbed off the wagon, went around to the back, and removed his saddle and saddlebags.

Liam carried his goods back up to the front of the wagon, tossed them on the ground, and reached up to shake Mordecai's hand. "I hope to see you again," he said forthrightly. "I hope to find your daughter and persuade her to come home." It was the first time he'd told Scott of this ambition.

Mordecai mumbled something, apparently unable to think of anything to say.

"I may not succeed, but it would be a way of making things up to you. For putting you out, I mean. Eating your food and so on."

"You owe us nothing."

"Still, if I can do that for you, I'd be honored."

"If you could bring Deborah home, I'd be in your debt, Mr. Carrigan. Forevermore I would. But she's a stubborn young woman. She's rejected everything we taught her. That's the fact, though I never say it so plain in front of her mother and brothers. But it's the truth, and there's no point in varnishing it. She's a whore, and a lost and sad young woman. I miss her, but I'd forgive all she's done in half a moment if only she'd come back."

"Reckon she knows that?"

"I don't know. She won't see us to talk to us."

Mordecai Scott shook Liam's hand again, then brought the wagon around and began to drive away. Liam was picking up his saddle when Scott stopped, turned around in his seat, and said, "By the way, if you do find Deborah, she won't be using that name. She gave that up, too, when she turned her back on her upbringing. She uses a variety of names now, but most of the time she just goes by the name of Lilly."

23

The barkeep who had saved Joseph's bacon at that fateful moment of hesitation in the Long Branch was named Paul Ditty, and Liam already had pegged him as his kind of man: straightforward, pragmatic, and not hesitant to answer a question. Tough as leather, too, for he was already back at work against the strict orders of his physician.

"I know exactly who Lilly is," he said to Liam. "Why are you looking for her?"

"I've got personal reasons, and not the kind that most seek her out for."

"You don't aim to hurt her, do you?"

"No. I've got no quarrel with her. She's good at heart, I think. She had a good raising."

"You know her family?"

"I've met them. I'd like to bring her back to them. But if you see her, don't tell her that. She wouldn't favor the idea."

"I'll keep mum. But I ain't seen her lately. She may not even be in Dodge at the moment."

"She has been, very recently. I hope she hasn't moved on. If she is here, I'll find her."

"Listen, Mr. Carrigan, while I've got the chance to talk to you, I need to talk about your brother."

"He appreciates the help you gave him, by the way, and he's mighty sorry you got stabbed."

"That right? You couldn't tell it. Looked to me like he got hit with the freezes."

"Joseph? No, no."

"Anyway, that ain't what I want to talk to you about. You need to know that there's a strong rumor that somebody's after his hind end, and I mean serious."

"Who?"

"You know them thieves he killed at the freight station? Two of them were brothers. Last name of Bartlett."

"I heard that."

"Well, there's a third Bartlett brother. He wasn't there."

"Ah."

"Story among the whores is, he's swore to kill the man who killed his brothers. Story is, he's been in jail in St. Louis but he got out a few days ago."

"You think this is a real threat?"

"All I can say is, I'd take it seriously. Your brother needs to watch his back for a spell. Maybe longer."

Liam nodded. "Thanks for the warning."

"You'll be seeing him to tell him?"

"I'll be seeing him. And if you see Lilly . . ."

"I'll try to find out where she lives and get word to you. Where will I find you?"

"At the wagon works by day, the Arment Livery from about midnight on through morning. Or, in the earlier part of the evening, you'll find me with my brother, walking his patrol along with him."

"You're going to be a deputy too?"

"No. A back watcher. If there's somebody after my brother, they'll have to go through me to get to him."

"No," Joseph said firmly. "There's no need for it, Liam. You go walking my patrol with me, folks will call me yellow."

"It's always about how things will look and what people will say, ain't it? That's all you think about, Joseph. You got too much sorry, lousy pride, brother. The truth is, I'd be walking with you even if there was no threat. I can't think of a better way to find who I'm looking for."

Liam had already described his plan to Joseph. "So you figure I attract harlots, is that it?"

"No. But you poke your nose into the right places to find them. I hit enough saloons and so on, I'll eventually find her if she's here to be found."

"You could do that without me."

"Yes, but why not do it with you instead? I like your company, though I can't always figure out why, and if there is a threat against you, there's nothing wrong with brothers helping each other out. That's been the way in this town with the Mastersons and the Earps already. We're just continuing the tradition. Besides, I've got to be on the lookout for Mack Stanley myself. We stick together, we can watch each other's back while I'm trying to find Lilly."

"I suppose it won't hurt." Joseph grinned. "To tell the truth, I'll be glad to have you along."

There was only one problem with Liam going on patrol: He wasn't a fast walker, given his injured ankle and the bullet furrow in his leg. But he was doing better on this, the third night of their common patrolling, than he had the first.

So far there had been no incidents. No sign of Mack Stanley, no increase in rumors of a visit from the remaining Bartlett brother.

In fact, it had been quite boring. Until this night.

The notification had come from a breathless hotel clerk who had run the equivalent of two miles of alleyways and streets, trying to find a lawman to report the brawl under way in a third-floor hotel room. By the time the rotund fellow located Joseph, he was so out of breath that it took two minutes for him to make himself understood.

"Somebody's going to be dead," he gasped out. "It may be too late already. I never heard such fighting and cussing."

Joseph being the lawman, it was his duty, not Liam's, to respond. He set off at a lope and quickly left his brother behind. But Liam followed as quickly as he could, and rounded a corner in time to see Joseph enter a hotel lobby. Liam trotted down the boardwalk and followed him.

The fight was still going on. Liam ran, sort of, up the stairs, wincing every time his ankle twisted. When he reached the upper hallway, Joseph was pounding on a door and threatening to kick it in if it wasn't opened. The fight continued at full rollick on the other side.

"Need some help?" Liam said.

"Maybe," Joseph replied. "I'm going to have to kick this door in. Unless you want to do it."

"Given the soreness of my ankle, I'll leave the kicking to you. I wish I had a pistol with me."

"I can't bend the rules of the law just because you're my brother. It's one thing to walk around on my patrol like you're a lawman, but another to carry arms when you're just a private citizen." Joseph hammered on the door again. "You in there! Quit the fighting and open up! Deputy marshal here!"

This time he seemed to have gotten their attention. The ruckus diminished.

Joseph hammered the door again. "Open up!"

The fighting stopped. Liam and Joseph glanced at each other; Joseph gave a little shrug.

The door rattled and opened. A burly, red-faced man as bald as a billiard ball stuck his head out. "What do you want?"

"To stop a murder," Joseph replied. "Sounds like one is about to happen in there."

"Hell, we're just having a dispute. Nothing serious."

"Who's the one you're disputing with?"

Another man stepped into Joseph's line of view. He was as big as the first man, but with thick hair and a drooping mustache. "That's me."

"What are you fighting over?"

"Money," the first man said. "He owes me some and says he don't."

"You two friends?"

"He's my brother-in-law."

"My name's Carrigan. I'm a deputy marshal here. I want to talk to you both. Seems to me this can be worked out without anybody getting hurt."

"Carrigan . . . the one who wiped out that gang?"

"Yeah. But let's not talk about that. Let's talk about your problem. You fellows about scared the clerk to death, you know. He thought somebody was going to die up here."

"He *will* die if he don't pay what he owes me!"

"Nobody's going to die. Let's go inside, sit down, and talk this out."

They all went into the room and closed the door behind them. Liam went along, seating himself beside a window where he could keep one eye on the street and another on Joseph. Watching his brother at work here just might prove to be entertaining.

One of the men started to quiz Joseph about the shooting at the freight station. Whether he liked it or not, that incident was going to follow Joseph the rest of his days. Probably it would be written up in the lore of western law enforcement a century from now.

Liam looked out over the town of Dodge. Not much to see, though. Just an empty section of street below, a few shops closed for the night and, across the alley, the top of the next building.

Liam was about to turn away when a movement caught his attention. A figure came clambering up over the edge of the adjacent roof. Another followed. The first figure was that of a man. The second was Lilly.

He'd found her! By sheer luck, or the destiny that Joseph was so fond of talking about, he'd finally found Deborah "Lilly" Scott.

Joseph had just steered the conversation away from his gunfight and around to the subject of the supposedly owed money. Tempers were rising again; one of the brothers-in-law was cussing now, threatening the other's life despite Joseph's repeated reminders that all this was being said in front of an officer of the law.

The pair began shouting at each other. One lunged at the other and Joseph jumped between them, pushing them apart. He glanced toward Liam, hoping for help, but Liam's eyes were locked on the window.

Joseph managed to push both the antagonists back, shoving one into a chair and the other onto the bed. He aimed long fingers at both. "Sit still! I didn't come here to fight you or to let you kill each other! We're going to settle this like peaceable men!"

Liam was on his feet now, still staring out the window. Joseph couldn't help but wonder what he saw that was so intriguing.

Liam was hardly aware of Joseph's problems. He was watching Lilly and the man with her, from whom she was taking a bottle that she turned up for a drink. The man was teetering on his feet, so drunk that Liam was surprised he'd been able to climb up the fire ladder to the rooftop. If this man had carnal intentions for his companion, he'd not have much luck at that level of intoxication unless he was a better man than most.

Even though Liam knew full well what Lilly was and could easily guess all the kinds of things she had done, it bothered him deeply to see her with a man. He didn't think of her now as Lilly the whore but as Deborah Scott the wayward but still-loved daughter.

Maybe he should get over there.

Lilly had given the man the bottle and was encouraging him to drink. Liam figured out what she was doing: It was easier to get him passed out on the roof and take his money from his pocket than to actually have to fulfill the physical part of their agreement.

The man took a swallow and put the bottle down. He moved toward Lilly and tried to kiss her, but she dodged him, swooped down, and picked up the bottle again. She took a small swig, then put it to his lips and tipped it up, feeding him so much liquor he turned away, choking.

She made him drink again and again. The volume of alcohol this man was consuming at such a fast rate was alarming, and Liam began to fear the fellow might poison himself with the alcohol. Liam had known a man who had done that very thing and died of it.

The man passed out and flopped over backward. Lilly stood over him, trying to stir him to see what would happen. Nothing did. He was out cold.

Liam expected to see her rifle through the man's clothes for money; surprisingly, she didn't. Instead she took the bottle and went to the front of the building and looked out over the raised facade. She tilted the bottle up and took a swallow, then set it on the wall, buried her face in her hands, and cried, her shoulders heaving.

Liam watched in puzzlement. What was wrong with her? Surely she wasn't crying because her partner had passed out. It had been very evident that she was try-ing to bring that about.

She picked up the bottle, took a long swig, and tossed it away behind her. It shattered, spattering the remainder of its contents over the flat rooftop.

Then Lilly put a foot up on the top of the facade and clambered up. She stood there, looking down at the street three stories below, and raised her arms like a diver.

Liam felt a cold hand close around his heart as he comprehended what she was about to do.

The argument Joseph was trying to referee erupted again at that moment and rose to a new level. The antagonists were on their feet again, and Joseph was again between them, his voice also growing louder.

Liam wheeled and headed for the door, but Joseph and the two arguing men were in his way.

"Settle down, both of you!" Joseph was demanding.

There was no time for words. As Liam pushed between the men, his fists shot out in opposite directions, catching both men in their jaws. They grunted in tandem and collapsed in such a corresponding fashion that it appeared to be choreographed.

Joseph gaped at the two unconscious men at his feet. "Liam, what the devil—"

But Liam was already out the door and loping down the hall toward the stairs.

24

Liam pounded out of the front door, oblivious to the pain in his ankle and leg. He ran out onto the street and felt overwhelmed with horror when he saw she was no longer standing on the top of the facade. He looked at the ground below it: She was not there either. Nor was she on the top of the covered porch that was roughly beneath the place she had stood.

She must have decided not to jump. Liam ran on into the alley and found the fire ladder. He climbed it to the roof as fast as he could.

She was seated now, leaning back against the rear of the facade and crying again. Liam felt relieved, then noticed that she had picked up the broken-off neck of the whiskey bottle she had tossed. She was pressing the jagged edge against her wrist.

The drunken man was still passed out cold where he had fallen.

"Deborah," Liam said.

She sucked in her breath and looked up sharply, not having noticed him climbing onto the roof. Now she gazed at him with fear at an animal level, backing up against the facade in a standing position and looking at him as if he would surely kill her.

"Why did you call me that name?" she asked. "My name is Lilly!"

"No. It's Deborah Scott. Your mother's name is Laurel and you have two brothers, Timothy and Leroy. Your father is Mordecai Scott, and they all live in a sod house some miles away from here. And they all miss you and wish you were home."

She stared at him, tears streaming down her face, then threw her head back and laughed. "Wish I was home! Oh, God above! They wish I was home, do they?"

Liam stepped toward her, extending his hand. "Deborah, please let me have that broken bottle. You're making me mighty nervous with it."

"Don't call me Deborah. Deborah is dead and gone. I'm Lilly. And Lilly will be dead soon enough. Why the hell are you here, anyway? How did you know I was up here?"

"I saw you from the window of the hotel over there. I saw you climb up on that wall. I thought you were going to jump."

"I was . . . but I couldn't: I'm afraid of falling. But I can cut myself. If I cut my wrist . . ."

"Deborah . . . Lilly . . . why are you so sad? Why do you want to die?"

She seemed to deflate. "Because I've got a baby in me."

Liam didn't expect to hear that, although later he would wonder why he was surprised. Prostitutes became pregnant every day.

"Well . . . then you'll need a home for that baby. Your family can help you. Come with me, Lilly. We'll get you to a doctor. I'll buy you some good food. If you want, we'll have your mother and father come see you. Or we can go to them . . . when you're ready. Don't hurt yourself, Lilly. Please."

"Why the hell should you care about me? I almost got you killed."

"Lilly, if that's the closest I come to getting killed, I'll be doing fine. It'll take more than Mack Stanley to kill me. Please don't cut yourself, Lilly. You'd be killing your baby right along with yourself. That baby is innocent. Don't do this."

"I just want to be dead."

"No you don't. Especially not with a family that loves you."

"They don't love me. How could they? I ran away. I started doing bad things. I'm a whore. That's all I am . . . a whore. How can a whore raise a baby?"

She jammed the broken edge of the bottle against her wrist, but lost her nerve and cast it away. She turned and crawled back up onto the top of the facade again, too quickly for Liam to get to her and stop her.

"Lilly, don't do it!"

"I just want to die. I can't birth a baby. I ain't fit to be a mother. I'm going to jump."

"Lilly, did you know that Timothy came looking for you?"

She stood unmoving, her back toward Liam. He crept closer a step or two, debating whether he could lunge and reach her before she could leap. He didn't dare try.

"He came to Dodge on foot, all the way from your old home. He wanted to take you home to see your mother because she wasn't feeling well and wanted to see her daughter again."

Lilly's shoulders heaved.

"What would I tell Timothy if you do this, Lilly . . . Deborah?"

"How do you know my family?"

"I visited them. I ate one of your mother's meals. I slept on blankets on the floor. I'll tell you all about it if you'll step down. Lilly, did you know that your father believes that you deserted the family because you are ashamed of his appearance?"

She frowned at him, a muddled, tired kind of frown. Then slowly she stepped down off the facade and sank to a seated position again, and hung her head in silence.

Liam walked over to her. "Everything will be well again. I'll take care of you. My brother Joseph will help me. He'll be glad to. He's a deputy marshal and he works at the livery too. I have a job at Drake Moore's wagon works. I don't make much money, but enough. We—my brother Joseph and me—will make sure you and your baby have what you need. If you want, we'll take you to—"

Liam stopped abruptly. Down below, Joseph was walking up the street, probably heading out to find medical attention for the two unconscious men in the hotel.

Behind him, though, was another man, moving toward him swiftly but in a covert manner. As Liam watched, the man drew his pistol.

"Joseph!" Liam yelled. "Joseph, behind you!"

Joseph turned, but it was too late. The man behind had the advantage and fired even before Joseph could realize he was there.

Joseph fell backward.

"No!" Liam screamed. "Joseph!"

He scrambled for the fire ladder.

Even as he descended, there was more shooting from the street. Liam was actually relieved to hear it: Dead men don't shoot.

Unarmed, unsure what he could do, but not even thinking about it under the circumstances, Liam came out of the alley and raced toward the gunman who had shot his brother. His bad ankle gave way, though, and he collapsed on the street short of reaching the man.

Liam looked up at the gunman just in time to see him jerk as Joseph shot him from a seated position three times in succession, every shot striking its target. The man did a strange dancelike spin and fell.

Liam got up and limped over to Joseph, who was managing to rise. "Joseph, are you hit?"

"I think so. . . . I don't know how bad." Joseph looked down at his side, which was growing red with fresh blood.

Liam tore his shirt open. "Thank God," he said. "It's not even as bad as the one I got on the leg. It just grazed the skin and broke it open. That's all."

Joseph nodded. He walked slowly over to the dead man. Other people, drawn by the gunfire, were beginning to approach. Joseph rolled the man over and looked at his face, the open eyes staring unseeing at the dark sky above.

"Do you know him?" Liam asked.

"No. But he bears a resemblance to a couple of those at the freight house."

"The third brother."

"Likely so."

"Joseph, do you know how close that one was? If I hadn't seen him when I did, you couldn't have known.

He'd have back-shot you and you'd have been dead before you knew it happened."

"I appreciate the shout, Liam. I owe you a very big favor. Did you come off the roof?"

"Yes."

"When did you go up there? And why?"

"Wait a minute and I'll tell you. I need to go back up there and get somebody."

Liam limped back to the alley and climbed the fire ladder rather gingerly, his ankle hurting more than it had the first time he went up. He reached the top and looked over.

The drunken man still lay like a fallen tree over on the other side of the roof, but Lilly was gone. She'd descended during the distraction of the shooting.

Liam was bitterly disappointed. He was sure she'd been ready to come with him. He had been on the verge of being able to fulfill his pledge to the Scott family.

Now she was gone, and he didn't even know where she lived. Or whether his admonishments and pleas would continue to carry any weight with her now that she was out of his presence. He feared for her life.

He descended the ladder to the street and rejoined his brother.

25

Home for Lilly was a small, cramped one-window room in a house that was little more than a shack. Two other rooms in the house had recently been occupied by other women, both of whom were in the same profession as Lilly. But time and fortune had brought bad things to those women and both were gone, one to her grave and the other to a hospital in Missouri, where she was being treated for one of the diseases of her trade.

So Lilly was alone in her dwelling now. She entered her room and cast herself onto her bed and lay there weeping, thinking how close she had come to taking her own life and feeling unsure whether it was good or bad that she had not actually done so.

She was haunted by the thought that young Timothy had come looking for her. It seemed inconceivable to her that anyone, even her own kin, could actually care about her. She was foul and ruined and evil, unworthy of love.

And now she was pregnant with a child whose father could be any of a number of men. A child probably conceived right on the very bed in which she now lay.

Closing her eyes, she vowed to God that she would sell her body no more. Whatever pressures life put upon her, she would not follow that path again. If only He would give her another chance, and give her child a chance.

Then she thanked God for Liam Carrigan. If not for his intervention, she would be dead. And as bad as life seemed, she was glad not to be dead. One person, her innocent little brother Timothy, still cared about her enough to come looking for her. Right now, that alone was enough to make life seem worth living.

Perhaps she should consider returning to her family, as Liam had urged. It seemed a radical step. She had despised life in that cramped, ugly house of dirt and poverty. She had been crushed under the restraints of the morality imposed upon her by her mother, and stressed by the isolation imposed upon them by her father's tendency to withdraw from the public world. But since leaving all that behind, she'd found no better things, only worse ones.

She would think about going back. Perhaps there was still a place for her at home.

Sleep came. For two hours she dozed, then awakened. She had heard a noise in the next room, a room that had been unoccupied since the death of the prostitute who had lived there. She opened her eyes, frowning, and listened closely. Footsteps. She sat up in her bed, terrified. Thoughts of ghosts came spilling in.

She heard the door next door squeak open. Footsteps . . . coming nearer. Then the door of her own room opened. Why hadn't she locked it? She pulled the covers up to her face and waited in terror to see who was entering.

"Lilly!" A man's voice. She relaxed just a little. At least it was a human being, not a phantom. "Lilly, are you in here?"

There was an odd quality to the speech that was familiar—the kind of speech pattern that comes from a lack of front teeth.

"Mack, is that you?"

"Yes, it's me. I been looking for you, Lilly. I need some help."

"I ain't whoring no more, Mack. I vowed to God this very night I'd give it up."

"That ain't why I'm here. I'm hurting. . . . I got a bullet wound and it's hurting me fierce. I need a place to rest and somebody to tend me a little. I'll pay you for it. . . . Just let me rest on your bed, sweetheart, and give me some food and so on for a day or two, until I'm better. I think the wound is getting putrid on me."

Lilly despised Mack Stanley: Even though he had been one of her better customers, she'd never liked the way he treated her. Never any respect or courtesy. He'd usually just called her "girl," hardly ever addressing her as "Lilly."

Now that he was hurt, he was crawling in all humble and pleading, calling her by name, calling her "sweetheart". . . . It riled her. She wondered how long the sweetness would last. Probably as long as it took for him to get to feeling better. Then he'd be back to his old mean self.

He was already inside and she knew there would be no turning him away. Rising, she lit a lamp and cranked it up. Mack made for her bed and collapsed onto it.

He stank terribly. There was more to it than his usual stench from failure to wash. Lilly was revolted. She knew what it was: His wound was going bad, as he had surmised. She went to the window and opened it wide. Fresh air spilled in, blowing the bedsheet curtains and making Stanley's reek a little easier to endure.

"Let me see how bad hurt you are," she said.

"The bullet just clipped right through me," he said. "It made a clean tunnel here in my side. I don't know why it went bad on me. It was the kind of wound that should heal fast."

"Did you wash it out with anything?"

"No." He was pulling up his shirt; the bad smell was getting stronger. "I didn't do nothing to it. Ain't seen a doctor, either."

Lilly put her hand on her nose, brought the lamp

near him, and looked with disgust at the infected, pinched bullethole. She didn't bother to ask him how or why he'd been shot. He probably wouldn't tell her, and the truth was, she didn't much care.

"Get me some whiskey, Lilly," he said. "I need a drink, and I figure if I can wash the wound out with whiskey, it might get better."

"You pour whiskey in that and you'll think there's been a fire built inside of you," she said. "How old is that wound?"

"Three days, I think. Maybe four. I don't remember."

"You need a doctor."

"No. No doctor. A doctor would talk to the law. I don't want to be answering a bunch of questions."

"I ain't got any whiskey."

"Then go out and buy some!" he snapped at her, a little of his usual self coming through. "You got money?"

She did have a little, earned from trysts with three cowboys the day before. But she didn't want Mack to know about it. "I'm clean broke," she said.

He cussed and pouted, then dug into his trouser pocket and pulled out some money. "Here . . . and don't you spend it on nothing but whiskey. And maybe a little food, if you can find it. Something easy to keep down. Since my wound started going bad on me, I can't keep my food down much."

Where would she find food at that time of night?

The saloons had little to offer. Maybe she could round up a few crackers somewhere. She didn't have a bite of food in her room.

"I've got a baby in me," she announced. "Did you know that, Mack? I've got me a baby inside. You might be the father."

"I don't give a damn about any baby of a whore. Get rid of it like you whores usually do. Why tell me about it? Right now all I want is some whiskey to wash this wound. And to drink. It's the only way to kill the pain."

She threw a shawl over her shoulders, took the money, and left. It angered her that she'd been intruded upon and now was being turned into a maid and errand girl. She wanted to defy him, but Mack scared her enough to make her comply: She knew how mean he could be.

Lilly owned no watch and did not know what time it was. All she knew was that it was late at night and that all the proper parts of the town were sleeping and dark. The improper parts, though, would still be going full tilt. Many a saloon and dance hall operated around the clock.

She walked up the street where the shooting had happened earlier. She had witnessed it from the rooftop, just before she'd made her exit and gone home. Having nothing to do with her, the shooting held little interest for her in and of itself. Liam Carrigan had been awfully interested, though. She'd heard him call the name Joseph. His brother's name, wasn't it? For Liam's sake she hoped that Joseph was not hurt. Right now Liam seemed a saint to her, a man of deep goodness who had given her hope at a moment she'd been so despairing that she was ready to die.

Lilly wasn't sure why she'd fled the rooftop. She probably should have stayed there and let Liam take her under his wing. If she had, she'd not be out right now, looking for whiskey for such a sorry specimen of humanity as Mack Stanley.

She supposed she'd run because she was scared, overwhelmed. Liam had talked so strongly about reuniting her with her family that he'd frightened her. When the opportunity to slip away during the distraction of the gunfight came, she'd taken it. Running away was her usual habit. She'd gotten good at it.

She headed for the nearest saloon, clutching her money, wishing she could use it to buy poison for Mack Stanley instead of whiskey. She despised the man. He'd tried to kill Liam Carrigan, a saint among men, the only human being besides her little brother who had shown an active interest in her welfare for the longest time.

She hoped Mack's wound would just keep on festering until it killed the scoundrel.

* * *

Normally at this hour Joseph and Liam Carrigan would both be soundly sleeping in their room at the livery. However, the shooting changed that pattern that night. As was usual when such events occurred, Charles Bassett had been brought in. Roused out of bed, he'd arrived to investigate and record what had happened. When one of his deputies killed a man, he wanted to know all the circumstances.

Bassett had taken complete statements from both Joseph and Liam. Liam's statement was of particular importance because he'd actually witnessed the events immediately preceding the fight, the approach of the gunman from Joseph's rear, the first shot fired, and Joseph's reaction.

Joseph's wound had been patched up by the local sawbones, who had also been gotten out of bed, though a little later, while Liam was giving his statement. Joseph's wound was very minor, and he was deeply grateful that the last Bartlett brother had been a poor shoot. Had he been better, Joseph could be on the undertaker's slab right now.

But there was still one more statement needed, that of the only other potential witness to at least part of the shooting. But Deborah "Lilly" Scott was not immediately at hand.

Bassett laid down his pen and stretched his cramped hand. He despised taking statements. Scanning over the document, he handed it to Joseph and had him read it. "Acceptable?" Bassett asked.

"Acceptable," Joseph replied, picking up the pen and signing his name at the bottom.

"There should be no ramifications from this shooting, which was clearly justified," Bassett said. "However, I do want the statement from this young woman. The fact that the both of you are brothers might cause some to suspect your statements are crafted to be protective. She would provide a degree of independent verification."

"I don't think she was positioned to see as much as I did," Liam said. "The latter part of the fight, though, she might have seen."

"I want her statement. Any idea where she could be found?"

"I don't know where she lives."

Bassett scratched his chin, then said, "Hold on just a minute. I'll be right back." He returned a minute or so later. "I just talked to Charlie Puncher in his jail cell. Charlie knows of Lilly and told me where she rooms. She might have returned there."

"I can go fetch her," Joseph said.

"You being involved directly in the shooting, I'd rather you stay put for now," Bassett said. "I'll go."

"Marshal, I felt like I gained her confidence this evening when I talked to her," Liam said. "If she sees the law coming, she'll just run off and hide. I think I could persuade her to come back."

Bassett shook his head. "Won't do. Someone could allege that during the time you fetched her back here unattended by any official law, you told her what to say in her statement. Best to let me do it. But if you have her confidence, your presence might be helpful. I'd appreciate it if you'd come with me."

"I'll do it, sir."

"Fine. Let's go."

Mack Stanley was waiting for Lilly when she returned with a bottle of cheap whiskey. "What the hell took you so long?" he asked as he snatched the bottle from her hand. He popped the cork and took a swig. "Yeah. Yeah. That's better." He winced and gingerly touched his wounded side. "God, that hurts." He took another swig.

"You want me to pour whiskey into the bullethole?" Lilly asked.

"Maybe. Not yet. It's swollen up right now. The hole's all closed up. Whiskey wouldn't go down into it. For now I'll just drink."

Lilly suspected that was all he'd ever intended to do. Mack Stanley was not a brave soul. Pouring alcohol into a wound was not something she could imagine him doing.

He lay back on her bed and drank from the bottle, staring at the opposite wall. His hair was sweaty and matted, his face pallid and sickly. The infection in the wound was beginning to make him a sick man.

Lilly sat on a broken chair in the corner and watched him drink. "You slosh that whiskey down your chin, now that your front teeth are gone," she observed.

This angered him. He aimed a finger at her. "Don't you mock me, girl! It's a damned sight hard enough to have a piece of trash like Liam Carrigan treat you in such a way to begin with! I ain't going to abide having a sorry whore mock me over it!"

"I wasn't mocking. Just noticing."

"Yeah. Yeah, well let it slosh down my chin. I don't care. I'll be settling my scores with Liam Carrigan soon enough. I almost got it done the other day, out west of town. He come into a saloon I was in, and I followed him out. We had us a little shooting party. I plugged him too. Shot him in the leg."

"Looks like he shot you back."

"You mocking me again?"

"I ain't mocking, I swear."

"Next time I'll shoot him in the damn head."

"He's a good man, I think," Lilly said.

"What did you say?"

"I said I think Liam Carrigan is a good man. He talked to me this evening."

"He was *here?*"

"No. I was up on a roof with him."

"You mean to tell me that you and him was going at

it? You told me when I come in that you don't do that now! You lying little harlot!"

"It wasn't that. I was up there with another man, who passed out, and he came up and talked to me. Know what he told me? He told me my little brother came to town looking for me. He told me my family is worried about me. They want me to be back with them. I think I might go."

"Yeah, you do that. Wait and see how they'll treat you when you birth out that baby you say you're carrying."

"They'll treat me fine. They always did. It was me who didn't do right by them. I can see that when I look back and am honest with myself. It's hard to be honest with yourself, you know."

Stanley took another swig and wiped the back of his hand across his mouth. "Why don't you just shut up? Whores ain't paid to talk. Hey, where's the rest of the money I gave you? This whiskey didn't cost as much as what I gave you."

"I'm keeping it. You told me you'd pay me if I took care of you."

"The hell you're keeping it! And the hell if I'll pay you a penny, girl! You'll take care of me or I'll snatch you bald-headed! I mean it!"

"I ain't giving that money back. I've got to make a living like anybody else."

Stanley set the bottle on the floor and got out of bed,

although it gave him evident pain to do it. He staggered around and faced her threateningly. She rose from her chair but still had to look up to see his face, glowering and glistening in the lamplight.

"I'll beat hell out of you, girl. I'll give you a set of front teeth to match mine. You want that. Huh?"

He drew back his fist. At just that moment, someone knocked on the door.

26

Stanley's eyes flashed fire. "What have you done, girl?" he snarled in a whisper. "Who the hell did you bring back here?"

"Nobody!" she said. "I swear!"

Another knock.

"Ask who it is!" Stanley whispered.

"Who's knocking?" she called out.

"It's me, Liam Carrigan. I'd like to talk to you some more."

Stanley for a moment looked terrified, then his anger overtook his fear and he grinned. "I'll be damned! So you two are going at it! I reckon I can guess what kind of 'talk' he wants!" Stanley reached under his jacket and brought out a small revolver. "I've got some talking of my own to do with him! Tell him to come in."

She shook her head. "No . . . no, I'll not do it. You'll shoot him!"

Liam called through the door, "What did you say, Lilly?"

"Call him in!" Stanley barked, a little too loudly. He grabbed Lilly and wrapped his arm around her neck, then backed up with her, positioning himself squarely against the open window.

"Who's in there with you, Lilly?"

Stanley jammed the pistol against her head. "Tell him to come in!"

"Mr. Carrigan," she called, her voice quavering, "don't come in! Mack Stanley's in here, and he's got a gun on me, and—"

The door burst open, shattering the latch and vibrating loudly on its hinges. Charles Bassett, having just kicked that door in, now leveled his pistol at Stanley's face. "Let her go!" he ordered.

"Won't do it!" Stanley bellowed. "Who the hell are you? Where's Carrigan?"

"I'm Town Marshal Charles Bassett. There's no Carrigan here."

"The hell! I heard his voice! I know his voice when I hear it!"

"Let her go."

"I won't do it!"

"Let her go, Mack!" It was Liam's voice, coming from behind Mack. Liam had circled around and gone to the open window. He held a small pistol that Bassett carried as a fallback weapon, which he'd slipped to Liam just before kicking in the door.

Mack Stanley, startled, wheeled around reflexively,

the move spinning Lilly around with him. His side was now exposed to Bassett. Stanley shoved his pistol out the window at Liam.

Liam and Bassett fired simultaneously, both shots hitting home. The bullets tore into Mack Stanley from either side. His arm around Lilly's neck suddenly went limp, dropping away as he collapsed to the floor. His eyes turned upward, glazed, and he was gone.

Bassett rushed into the room, pistol still pointed at Stanley, until he was sure the man was dead. He holstered the pistol. Liam was already scrambling in through the window. Once in, he put his arm around Lilly's shoulder.

"Are you all right, Lilly?"

"Yes," she said. "I want to go home."

"You *are* home, Lilly."

"No. My real home. I want to go home to my mother and father. Will you take me?"

"I'll take you."

Bassett drew in a deep breath and let it out slow.

"It's been quite a night in Dodge City," he said. "Quite a night."

The horse Liam rode had been bought at a bargain price from Caleb Arment. It was a fine mount and Arment had taken a bath in the transaction but didn't seem to mind it. In fact, he'd insisted on the low price. "I'm pleased to help out the brother of the finest employee I ever had, and the best deputy marshal who ever patrolled the streets of Dodge," he'd said proudly.

It was two weeks after the night Mack Stanley died that Liam and Joseph rode out to the sod house of the Scott family. Just a visit, paid in answer to an invitation from a grateful family. It would be the last such visit the Carrigan brothers would make before leaving Kansas to head for Montana, where they hoped to find their uncle.

Just now both brothers were in a frame of mind to get out of Kansas as quickly as possible. Kansas had given them more adventures, scrapes, close calls, and outright physical damage than either had ever anticipated.

"We're heading to Montana for our own safety," Liam joked to Mordecai Scott as they ate stew that both knew the Scotts couldn't really afford to feed them. That didn't matter, though: They'd already left a couple of hams and other foodstuffs in the family's storage dugout outside. Liam had managed to slip them in without being noticed. The Scotts would never have accepted the gifts if they knew about them.

Lilly didn't look like Lilly anymore. There was something quite different in her demeanor, her complexion, her eyes: It was a life that had not been there before . . . and the same was true of her mother. The woman seemed ten years younger, now that her straying daughter was home again, and Lilly herself seemed younger as well, almost childlike. Liam could hardly associate her with the prostitute he had known.

It was the best meal the Carrigan brothers could remember in a long time. When they readied themselves to leave, they did so with true reluctance and regret, and with promises that if they should ever be in Kansas again, they would look the family up.

"I want to talk to you, if I could," Mordecai said to Liam as he was about to mount his horse.

"Why, sure."

"Over here, where we can talk in private."

Liam nodded and handed the reins to young Timothy. He and Mordecai walked together over near the dugout. Liam wondered if Mordecai had spotted the hams and such and was about to diplomatically refuse them.

Mordecai looked down, collecting his thoughts a few moments before he began. "Liam, have you ever noted the birthmark on my hand?"

Liam nodded. "I have."

"It's a distinctive thing—not the most distinctive thing about me . . . but it's a mark you could know me by, even if my face was normal."

"Yes," Liam acknowledged. He wondered what this was leading to. It was beginning to make him a little nervous.

"There's other people who have marks like that too. Some of them birthmarks like mine. Or maybe tattoos. Or scars . . . powder burns, maybe."

Liam nodded. His heart was pounding hard.

"There was a man I . . . met . . . quite a few years ago.

Met him in what you might call bad circumstances. That man is the one who ruined my face. A blast of shot from a smoothbore."

Liam could not speak.

"He had a mark on him. On his neck. I remember it well. It could be that . . . if I saw such a man, I'd know him. It might take me a day or two to recollect where I saw that mark before, but I'd know him. And it could be that he would remember me, too, for the mark on my hand."

"Could be. What do you think you might say to that man if you met him, Mordecai? Especially if that man told you how he regretted more than anything how things turned out that day, and how, if he could go back, he'd not—"

Mordecai wouldn't let him finish. "I think I'd tell that man that what happened happened in wartime, between two men fighting for their lives because that was what they were expected and obliged to do. That it wasn't nothing personal. Just war. Sorry, bloody, cruel, hellish war. And I'd tell him that war is long over. And thank God it is."

"Yes, indeed," Liam said. "Amen."

"And I'd tell that man he need not bear any burden for what happened to me. What happened just happened. And I'd tell him not to worry: Even a man with a ruined face he has to hide behind a mask can know a lot of happiness." He looked over toward Deborah, who was talking quietly with her mother, her arm over her shoulder. "Especially now."

Liam's eyes were red and moist. It was harder to talk than ever. "I think that man would like to hear those things," he managed to reply.

"There's one final thing I'd tell him—the most important thing of all," Mordecai said. "I'd tell him that there were some years during which I despised him, not even knowing who he was, where he was, or even if he was still alive. I despised him just knowing what he'd done to me. But those years of despising, like the years of the war, are past. So I'd tell him that everything is all right now." He paused. "I'd tell him that I forgive him."

All Liam could do was nod.

"Liam!" Joseph called. "Time to go. We've got a lot of traveling ahead."

Liam nodded and waved at his brother. When he looked back at Mordecai, his hand was extended.

Liam accepted it. The two men shook hands and said no more to one another. Liam walked away, mounted his horse, and raised a hand to wave at the Scotts one final time, with an extra wave just for Deborah.

"Ready to go?" Joseph asked.

"Ready to go," Liam replied.